HEARTS *of* AMISH COUNTRY™

KEEPER *of* HER HEART

Anita Greene

Annie's®
AnniesFiction.com

Library of Congress-in-Publication Data
Keeper of Her Heart/ by Anita Greene
p. cm.
I. Title
                    2017952631

AnniesFiction.com
(800) 282-6643
Hearts of Amish Country™
Series Creator: Shari Lohner
Series Editor: Janice Tate

10 11 12 13 14 | Printed in China | 9 8 7 6 5 4 3 2

"*Ach*, Fannie. You're a terrible sight."

Fannie Lapp looked at Sarah's pristine dress and then down at her own faded purple dress. It was her oldest one and was tatty from wear and constant washings. Pieces of hay clung to the hem. Her gray work apron had mended tears overlapping mended tears, and odorous bits of barnyard were stuck to her black shoes.

Jabbing the tines of her pitchfork into the soiled hay, she swallowed back an unkind retort, choosing instead to state the obvious. "I'm cleaning the goat barn." Someone had to do it. For one fleeting moment, Fannie tried to imagine Sarah wielding a pitchfork as musty hay dust danced in the air. The mental picture would not form. Her cousin had avoided the chores that took place outside the *Haus* since childhood.

Sarah Yoder huffed in irritation. Heavy with child, she took care climbing down from the spring wagon. "Help me unload these things." The ties of her white organdy *Kapp* fluttered in the crisp morning air. "*Mamm* says they are to go into the washhouse attic."

Because Sarah was eight years older than Fannie, she gave the orders and Fannie carried them out. That was the way life had been from the moment Fannie came to live with Aunt Susie and Uncle Will following the death of her parents when she was five.

Fannie lowered the tailgate and removed *Grossdawdi's* rocking chair and washstand. She ran her hand over the well-made pieces. Her fingers dipped into the dings and across the scratches accumulated over the years.

Sarah carried a washing bowl and pitcher up the squeaky stairs leaving Fannie to manage the furniture.

Favoring her bad hip, Fannie lifted the spindle-legged washstand. She stopped at the door and dragged the soles of her shoes across the boot scraper before following her cousin up the stairs.

Sarah stood in the center of the small room with a wry look on her face. "Are they expecting royalty?"

The room was painted linen white. A narrow bed stood in one corner with a rag rug on the floor beside it. The bed frame and matching chest of drawers were oiled to a brilliant sheen. Above the small wooden desk, a calendar from the feed store was tacked to the wall. A straight-backed chair was tucked beneath the desk where a kerosene lamp sat ready to use.

"This is nicer than any hired man's room I've ever seen. Is that one of your quilts, Fannie?"

She wondered how many hired men's rooms Sarah had actually seen, but pushed the question aside. "*Jah.*" The quilt in question was a neat blend of brown and tan. The quilt had been Fannie's project two winters ago. She didn't dare approach the bed lest the stink of the barnyard find its way into the nine-patch quilt. "The colors and pattern are right for this room."

Aunt Susie had hired a new man after their *Englischer* neighbor, Leland James, quit so he could devote his time to his infirm wife. In the meantime, the work of caring for their small herd of Alpine goats had fallen on Fannie.

Sarah's eyes narrowed. "I think Mamm and Aunt Lucy are up to something." She tapped her finger against her perfect pink lips.

Fannie forced herself not to fidget beneath her cousin's shrewd gaze. She'd had the same disquieting thought. Her aunts were oddly tight-lipped about the man they had hired.

"Ach *vell*." Sarah slapped her hands against her thighs. "No time to figure it out." She descended the stairs. Fannie followed on her heels. At the bottom, Sarah turned and shook her finger at Fannie. "You be careful." Sarah's blue gaze was fixed on Fannie's cheek with its old, puckered scar. "Don't let them talk you into a pity match with a poor, down-on-his-luck man. You don't want that!"

Fannie's heart tumbled in her chest. Around the town of Winsome, the whispers would follow her forever. *Poor Fannie. She had to take what she could get.* Such a fate would be worse than being a *Maedel* like her Aunt Lucy. Unmarried. No husband or children to call her own.

Sarah walked past the rocking chair Fannie still had to carry up the stairs. "You'll figure out what they're up to and do the right thing, Fannie. You're sensible enough."

Sensible. Why did people offer up being sensible like a consolation gift to replace the heart's dearest dream?

Sarah climbed into the wagon, puffing from the baby's added weight. "Finish the barn chores, then change your dress before Mamm's new hired man arrives. Otherwise, he'll think he's come to work for heathens." With a snap of the reins, she started old Tommy and went on her way back to the main Haus where she lived with her husband, Samuel, and their three children.

With her hands on her hips, Fannie stared at the rocking chair. "I should hope the hired man would be bright enough to realize I'm doing the work that is to become his."

"Move, Petunia." Fannie dodged the inquisitive goat and heaved the last of the soiled hay into the heaping wheelbarrow. Her hip no longer merely ached. The old injury burned like fire.

The herd queen, Daffodil, nibbled at her skirt while the kids leaped onto the loaded wheelbarrow as though it were a mountain. Their collar bells jingled in time to their antics.

"Scoot!" Laughing, Fannie pushed them away, but they came right back. "How will I ever get my work done?"

Fannie pushed the wheelbarrow out of the barn. The kids followed, jumping and bouncing on and off the heavy load. Marigold, the feistiest kid, frolicked across the field to join the fun. She jumped too high, sailed over the load and landed on the other side in a heap.

Setting the legs of the wheelbarrow down, Fannie rushed to where the kid sprawled in the dirt, looking mystified by what had happened.

"Silly girl." Fannie squatted down at her side. In a moment's time, she realized her mistake.

Hooves thumped onto her back and shoulder.

"Ach!" She raised her hand to keep the rambunctious goats away.

A large doe butted Fannie, knocking her to the side. Her head hit the wheelbarrow handle with a painful crack. She saw stars as she fell to the ground, surrounded by bleating goats and clanging bells. She shoved at the hairy bodies. Titus, the Great Pyrenees dog that guarded the herd, was clearly unhappy with the chaos and added his deep bark to the clamor.

A masculine voice intruded on the din.

Surprise raced through Fannie as two strong hands pulled her up off the ground.

Airborne, she clung to a crisp, white shirt. Blinking hard to clear her head, she looked up at her savior. Her breath stuck in her chest. The man smiling down at her couldn't be real. The bump on her head had created a hallucination.

"I hit my head."

"I saw that."

Hallucinations didn't speak, did they? "I must have hit it harder than I thought." The words came out in a breathy rush.

The figment of her imagination frowned. "Should I get a doctor?"

She tugged on the cloth she held in her hand, testing it to assure herself the fabric was real. Her mouth went dry. "Gideon Zook?"

He smiled exactly as she remembered. "Hello, Fannie Lapp."

Fannie's heart came back to life with a painful thump. He wasn't putting her down, so she wiggled.

He set her feet on the ground.

Brushing his hands from her arms, she wobbled before steadying herself. She put her hand to her face, an automatic gesture as old as the scar she covered. "You're here."

"I am. And apparently just in the nick of time."

Fannie stared at him, not knowing how to begin sorting out this phenomenon. Gideon Zook was eight years older than her twenty-two years. She knew that for a fact. Her ten-year-old self had counted every one of those years each time she saw him. And every time, she was disappointed by the math. There was no way around the facts. She was too young for Gideon to come courting.

And then he'd left Winsome.

Remembering how hurt she'd been caused a painful tightening in Fannie's chest.

Gideon had been a part of Sarah's teenage crowd. At the age of eighteen, he'd chosen not to be baptized into the church. He'd left the community, breaking the hearts of his family and friends. And Fannie.

"You left us." The accusation flew from her mouth before she could think to stop it.

"I did." His green eyes darkened beneath the wide brim of his hat and fringe of blond hair. "And that was a mistake."

Amazed by the remnant of hope bubbling up inside her after all these years, Fannie gave in to the fear of believing him. It couldn't be true. "Why are you here?"

"Susie Lapp hired me to work for her."

Fannie's knees gave out. He caught her arms and helped her sit on the handle of the wheelbarrow. The wheelbarrow filled with a load of stinky barn bedding.

Had she held onto her girlhood crush and foolishly dreamed of his return, she would have imagined a cart filled with sweet-smelling rose petals, and she would be wearing her Sunday dress. The reality seemed more fitting.

Gideon wore plain clothes. His cotton shirt was bright white, and his broadfall trousers were stiff with newness. He stood among the goats, not batting an eye at their inquisitive nibbling and bumping. Titus snuffled around his pant legs and shoes, and he didn't draw back an inch.

Certainty settled over her. "Aunt Susie and Aunt Lucy know they hired *you*? Gideon Zook?" This explained their silence on the subject of the new hired help.

"Leland told them who I was, but I made it clear in my letter too. I didn't want any surprises."

Miffed that even her Englischer neighbor was in on the secret, Fannie threw her hands up. "No surprises!"

He had the grace to look abashed. "Not with the adults, at least." An odd expression flickered across his features. "Except that you're an adult now too."

His recognition of that fact caused a flicker of possibility to set Fannie's heart aglow for a moment before she squelched the ember, unwilling to feed the flame. She had no illusions about herself. *Poor Fannie.*

Sarah was right. Somehow Gideon had fooled her aunts into hiring him. She couldn't love a man who had walked away from his family. Why had he come back? He hadn't truly answered her question.

Standing, she straightened her apron. "Come greet Aunt Susie and Aunt Lucy. They're mixing up a batch of soap."

Fannie led the way to the Grossdawdi Haus. She would watch him carefully. If he had come back to Winsome to take advantage of her elderly aunts, she would be sure to march him right back out again.

Gideon picked up the black duffel he'd dropped when he rushed to Fannie's aid. His twelve years in the English world had made him more forward than a woman like Fannie was accustomed to. In the future, he'd try to think before acting.

He trailed after Fannie, crossing a tidy strip of green lawn. Her gait was uneven, so he matched his steps to her slower pace. The buggy accident that took the life of her mother and father had left her with the limp and the scar on her cheek. He'd always thought of her—if he thought of her at all—as Sarah Lapp's shy little cousin. When he left Winsome, Fannie had been too young to capture his attention. But he was back in town, and little Fannie Lapp had grown up.

She had his attention now.

She led him past flower beds overflowing with yellow and red petunias. He removed his hat as he climbed the steps up onto the porch of the Grossdawdi Haus and followed Fannie into the kitchen.

Two elderly women stood side by side at the island counter with their backs to the door.

"Aunties. Gideon Zook is here."

The women turned.

Surprise speared through Gideon followed by amusement. He clamped his lips together to contain a chuckle.

The women goggled at him through the lenses of safety glasses.

"Ooooh. Ach. Gideon." Lucy Miller's lilting tones swept Gideon back in time. She had doted on every child she met. He and his friends used to flock to her for the peppermints she always carried. She lifted her goggles to sit on her brow above wire-framed spectacles.

Her sister, Susie Lapp, swept her own goggles down around her neck.

Both women came at him with arms outstretched. It was the kind of welcome he had dreamed of, but didn't dare expect.

"Look how you've grown." Susie shook his hand, patted his shoulder, and all but pinched his cheek.

"And dressed plain as a prophet." Lucy took his hat and pushed him into a chair at the kitchen table. A plate heaped with sugar cookies appeared in front of him. "Pour *Tay*, sister."

The aunts joined him at the table, filling the room with their good-natured chatter.

He wished Fannie would join them, but she had donned her own pair of goggles to finish the project her aunts had abandoned. At her nape, a wisp of dark-brown hair had escaped her Kapp.

Susie poured hot tea into his cup. "It's wonderful that you're here. Imagine our surprise when Leland said you were coming home."

Gideon thought he heard Fannie give a quiet snort.

Lucy's spoon clinked against the sides of her cup as she stirred in cream and an abundance of sugar. "Leland is a good man."

Gideon agreed. He had worked part-time for Leland James before leaving Winsome. The man was kind and generous. Though English, he was well-connected with the Amish community. When Gideon made the decision to return to the community, he had phoned Leland, knowing the man would help him secure a job. He didn't realize the job he'd be offered was the same one Leland was leaving.

"Leland said you've traveled." Susie leaned forward. "Have you been to Florida? I've always wanted to go to Florida."

"They have palm trees." Lucy chimed in.

"And dolphins, sister. I've always wanted to see a real dolphin." Susie took a cookie. "Did you go west? Did you see the Rocky Mountains?"

Gideon took refuge in eating the cookies that melted in his mouth and swilling tea as the sisters peppered him with questions they gave him no time to answer. During a momentary lull in their good-natured prattle, he glanced up and found Fannie's brown eyes focused on him. Without a word, she turned back to carefully weighing ingredients and whipping them up in a stainless steel bowl.

Unease prickled across his skin. Not everyone would be as happy to see him as her aunts.

"We have a room above the washhouse for you."

Lucy's declaration brought his attention back to the table.

"Fannie made the quilt. She's a fine quilter."

A sudden clatter at the counter startled Gideon.

Fannie moved quickly to contain whatever crisis had taken place.

He rose from his chair, intent on helping her, but Susie grabbed his sleeve.

"That room is only for the summer, mind. It has no heat. We'll figure out something more permanent before cold weather comes."

Winter. A shiver rippled up Gideon's spine. He came back hoping to rebuild what he'd once had in this small community. Living in the world beyond Winsome had been exciting, but none of what he had seen or done came close to replacing the love of his family. He wanted to mend his relationships with Mamm and *Daed* and his brothers, Joshua and Abram. For that to happen, he'd have to seek their forgiveness.

His heart pounded at the thought. Some things were harder to forgive than others. As much as he wanted to get back into the good graces of his own family, it was the death of his friend, Jacob King, that haunted him. Forgiveness from Jacob's family would give him the peace he longed for.

Gideon took another sugar cookie. He hoped he was still here when winter came.

2

Fannie raised the dark-green shade and pushed up the lower sash, opening the window two inches. A light pitter-patter of rain tapped on the glass. Her second-floor bedroom held the warmth of the day, making it difficult to fall asleep. Nights like this were when the memories of the buggy accident tormented her the most.

The weather had been rainy that night too. She'd been sitting on Mamm's lap. The *swish* of the buggy wheels skimming over the wet road and the *clip-clop* of the horse's hooves had lulled her to sleep.

The peace had been broken by Daed's hoarse shout. Fannie had opened her eyes and seen a bright light surround the carriage moments before a sickening roar filled the night air. Ripped from Mamm's arms, Fannie had been flung into the ditch on the roadside. Her next memory was of several men in uniforms leaning over her and talking in English.

Fannie rubbed her hand across the tough skin of the scar that curved across her cheek.

After several frightening hours alone in the hospital, Aunt Susie and Uncle Will had come and told her a speeding car had hit the buggy from behind. Her Mamm and Daed had been killed in the accident, and she would be going home with them to live.

Fannie wiped a stray tear from her cheek and tossed the heavy length of her braid back over her shoulder. She took a moment to breathe in the damp night air and listen to the chirp of crickets and the trill of tree frogs. She'd been taught from a young age to accept the life she had been blessed with, but the memories always made her long for her parents and the life she never got to live with them.

Fannie pulled her thoughts away from the past and back to the present. The nanny goats had not yet been driven into the barn by the shower. Their bells clanged and tinkled as they moved between the pasture and the barn. Petunia's bell chimed in the distance. That mischievous girl was browsing at the far end of the field among the leafy bushes. Somewhere out there, Titus kept watch—a lone sentinel faithfully guarding his herd.

The bleating of the kids came from the barn where they were confined to the weaning pen through the night with a rack of alfalfa hay. They would be allowed access to their mothers after the morning milking.

Fannie's gaze wandered to the washhouse. The attic window was dark.

Gideon Zook's appearance had shattered the quiet routine of her day. He'd set her heart pounding, and that was unsettling. Years ago, he'd turned his back on all she held dear. She couldn't imagine walking away from her family or the community.

She rested her arms on the windowsill. Why had he chosen to work for her aunts? They were wonderful people, but his family farm was close by in the same church district.

Gideon's eldest brother, Joshua, had married a girl from an Indiana settlement. He'd moved there to take over her father's farm. That had happened before Gideon left Winsome.

His youngest brother, Abram, had taken over working the home place for his Mamm and Daed. There was always more than enough work on a farm. Why had Gideon come here instead of going there to help Abram?

Fannie covered a yawn. Morning always came early. Time to set aside the unanswerable questions and get some sleep. She left the window open and climbed back into bed. Twisting and turning, she found the sweet spot in the center of the mattress where her hip no longer ached. She relaxed to the soothing music of the night and drifted off to sleep.

Sharp, urgent barking woke Fannie. She rubbed a hand across her face trying to dispel the fog of sleep.

The barking came through the open window again. Titus was sounding the alarm. Something was wrong.

She rolled to the edge of the bed and snatched yesterday's dress off the footboard where she'd draped it. Her fingers fumbled with the fabric.

Titus became frantic. A cacophony of barking, bleating, and bells came through Fannie's open window.

Barefoot, she hurried down the stairs and into the kitchen. Her aunts were already there. Their gray hair was wound about their heads in braided halos and their robes had been hastily tied.

"Take this." Aunt Lucy handed Fannie a huge flashlight.

Aunt Susie held out a plastic bag. "Here are treats in case you need them."

"*Danke.*" Fannie pulled on her raincoat and shoved her feet into a pair of knee-high rubber boots and clumped her way to the door. The rain had begun to come down in earnest. She pulled up her hood and hurried down the steps.

The racket came from the far side of the pasture. Fannie's pulse quickened. The hitch in her gait made running difficult. As a child, she'd wished for wings to keep up with the other children on the school playground. She again wished for those wings so she could fly as she crossed the yard to the pasture gate.

Titus no longer sounded urgent, but his low *woof* held an anxious note.

Entering the edge of the pasture where the goats loved to browse, Fannie muscled through the low brush. Wet leaves swished across her face and branches snagged on her hood and pulled at her coat.

Overhead lightning flashed. In its eerie glow, she caught a glimpse of a shadowy figure leaning over Titus. Uncertainty ran jagged through her. Lifting her flashlight high, she stepped from the brush and aimed the strong beam of light into the darkness.

Gideon.

She stared at him, catching her breath. The soaking rain plastered his hair to his head. He had no coat. The fabric of his shirt clung to him like a second skin. He'd done up the middle three buttons—enough to claim decency. He had lifted one suspender over his shoulder while the other dangled at his hip. He hadn't bothered with socks.

He raised his arm to ward off the bright beam of light. "Fannie?"

She stepped closer.

Titus came to her, whining and anxious. His wet coat of fur lay flat, making him look smaller.

"What happened?" She had to shout to be heard above the splash of the rain and the distant rumble of thunder.

"You have escapees. Will they come if you call them?"

"They should." She desperately hoped stale oatmeal cookies tasted better than freedom.

Gideon bent low. "The fence is down. Be careful where you step." He held the wire so she could walk through the gap.

A shallow ditch separated the pasture from the road. Fannie took care not to step into it and become a casualty of the night's escapade as she called out, listening for the answering bells. She called again, straining to hear.

She heard their bells over the rain before finding them with the beam of light. Petunia jumped across the ditch followed by Bluebell. Candytuft couldn't make the distance. Her hind feet splashed into the water at the bottom ditch. Panicked, she flailed about, then found her footing, climbed out, and joined the others.

Fannie fed the nannies tidbits of oatmeal cookie, leading them back through the hole in the fence. She handed the flashlight to Gideon before giving the goats more cookie crumbs. She added petting and head scratches to their reward for coming when called. "How did the fence come down?"

Gideon shined the light over the silvery glint of the wire. "Looks like someone cut it."

The shock of disbelief jolted through Fannie's midsection.

Tugging on the fence, he moved the light over the ground as though searching for something. "Let's get them out of the rain. I'll fix the fence in the morning."

"Come on, girls." Fannie wiped the rain from her face and started back for the barn. The three wayward adventurers followed closely, nudging the pocket where she had tucked the treats.

Gideon stayed at her side, holding branches out of the way and guiding her with the beam from the flashlight. Titus brought up the rear. He held his sodden tail high over his back as he snuffled through the leaf litter.

They reached the barn door as a flash of lightning lit up the sky.

Fannie got them into the barn, relieved none of them balked and decided a chase around the pasture would be the perfect ending to a less than perfect night. They joined the does who'd wisely come in out of the rain. The goats milled about in the barn's open space, and she counted noses to be sure everyone was safely inside.

In the weaning pen, the kids bleated and climbed over each other in an effort to join their mothers. They would eventually give up as they were separated from them by double fences with a walkway in between.

Dispensing the rest of the treats, Fannie ran her hands over the fine, coarse hair of the daredevils, checking for injuries. Not finding any, she shooed Tulip off one of the small benches in the loafing area and sat. She pushed back the hood of her coat. A drop of water landed on her neck and slid beneath her collar, sending shivers up her spine.

Gideon sat next to her looking bedraggled. His hip brushed her skirts. "The kids are putting up quite a fuss."

Fannie sighed. "They'll calm down. All of them have begun eating the alfalfa in the rack."

"You okay?" His gaze flicked to her leg, then back to her face.

Heat traveled up Fannie's neck. "Jah. This is the first time they've ever escaped. I check the fence often too."

A smile played across his lips. "Don't be hard on yourself, Fannie. The goats had help. Titus did a good job letting us know there was trouble."

His use of the word *us* sent a zing of awareness through her that she chose to ignore. "Perhaps teens were out playing pranks tonight."

Gideon shrugged into his other suspender. "Do you have extra fencing?"

"In the storage shed behind the barn."

"I'll have the hole patched before you finish the morning milking, okay?"

"Danke."

Bluebell bumped her head against Fannie's thigh, insisting on attention. Fannie obliged, breathing in the aroma of sweet hay mingled with the masculine scent of Gideon.

Fingering her braid, she glanced at him from beneath her lashes. "Danke again for your help."

"You're welcome. It's why I'm here."

The tiny bubble of happiness close to her heart deflated as though pricked with a pin. Helping her was his job. Nothing more. Nothing less. "My aunts will be waiting to hear what happened."

He stood. "Ready to make the dash for the house?"

"Jah." She led him through the milking parlor and milk room to the door closest to the house.

Opening the door, he looked out at the sheets of rain coming down. "On the count of three."

Fannie raised the hood of her coat and nodded. Another bolt of lightning flashed across the sky.

He waited for the thunder to rumble, said a fast, "One, two, three," and yelled, "Now!"

Fannie dashed from the barn, her raincoat flapping about her knees and her boots splashing through puddles. Realizing he wasn't beside her, she looked back over her shoulder.

He'd paused to throw the latch on the door and was racing to catch up.

Fannie swung back around and stumbled. "Oof!" In an instant, she lay prone in the grass, the smell of wet earth in her nose.

Gideon skidded to his knees beside her. "Are you hurt?"

"I'm okay." With his help she sat up, the ground squishy beneath her hands.

"Let me help you up."

She took his hand, so much larger than hers. The warmth of his skin sent a tingle up her arm. Surely, her breathlessness was due to her fall, though the universe suddenly centered on her hand and the strong fingers wrapped around it.

"Here we are."

She let him pull her up the porch steps she didn't remember running toward. Embarrassed by her response to him, she felt anxiety slice through her.

He squeezed her fingers bringing her gaze back to him. "You okay?"

Before she could answer, the kitchen door swung open.

"Here they are." Aunt Lucy stepped back. "Come in. You, too, Gideon. We have hot Tay. Don't want you to catch a chill."

Directly overhead, lightning flashed. The roll of thunder followed immediately.

Gideon gestured Fannie through the door and followed her inside. He stood on the doormat letting the worst of the rainwater drip from the hem of his trousers.

"Here you go." Susie handed him a plush towel.

"Thank you." He dried his hair, face, and neck.

Fannie took off her raincoat and hung it on a hook by the door. Her braided hair ran down her back like a river of dark molasses, the tip swinging with each step she took. Her limp was more pronounced now.

He followed her to the table. "Did you get hurt when you fell?"

She slumped into a kitchen chair. "I think I skinned my knee."

Tossing the towel over the back of a chair, Gideon squatted in front of her. "Let me see."

She gasped and pulled her skirts tight about her legs. "*Nee.*"

Gideon bolted upright. Heat rushed up his neck. "I-I'm sorry." *Fool.* Nice Amish girls didn't go around showing their knees to people, especially not to manly people.

Susie rushed out of the room, calling out, "Lucy, I'll get your salve and bandages."

He slid into the chair where he'd deposited the towel, berating himself for forgetting so soon to act more circumspect around Fannie.

Lucy placed a hot cup of tea in front of him. "Drink this."

He took a sip and nearly choked. Whatever she'd put in the cup, it wasn't regular tea.

"I steeped it extra long, so it's real strong." She smiled at him before bustling off to make a cup for Fannie.

Her cheeks pink, Fannie leaned forward and whispered, "How bad is it?" She glanced at his teacup.

He grimaced. "Pretty bad. What is it?"

Fannie shrugged. "Some herbal concoction."

Susie bustled into the room carrying an old shoe box. "I have your first-aid supplies, sister."

"*Gut.*" Lucy walked over to the table with a cup of tea for Fannie.

Setting the shoe box on the table, Susie took the lid off. "Everything should be here."

Lucy shuffled through the contents, pulling out gauze patches and tape in packaging that looked like it had been around since Eisenhower was president. Wielding a lethal-looking pair of scissors, she pulled a chair around and sat in front of Fannie.

Fannie and her aunts looked at Gideon.

"What?"

Fannie made a stirring motion with her finger.

"Oh." Gideon shifted sideways in his seat so his back was to her.

This was so completely ridiculous he had to hold back the laughter tickling his stomach to get out. "You know, I've seen knees before." He wasn't sure if Susie's snort was a suppressed chuckle or a sign of disgust. "Actually, I have *two* of them." This time he was sure she was laughing. "I think if you've seen one knee, you've seen them all." Which wasn't the complete truth, but the alternative to talking was drinking the noxious brew in his teacup.

Susie asked, "Why was Titus upset?"

"Three of the nannies got out." Fannie hissed in pain.

Gideon looked over his shoulder. His glance was met with dark-brown eyes flecked with golden fury. He turned back to face the counter. "Someone cut the fence wires."

Both aunts gasped in unison.

"All the goats are locked up in the barn, no worse for the adventure." Fannie's voice had an edge.

Wondering if that was a message for him to hush his mouth, he risked another glance over his shoulder. Sure enough, she shook her head once and glared at him. *Okay, then. Message received.*

When he was finally allowed to turn around, the dark-brown liquid in his cup had turned cold.

Susie and Lucy flitted around the kitchen like two elderly angels in braided halos, chattering away in Pennsylvania Dutch. When their flight paths crossed, they would whisper and giggle before going separate ways again.

Not wanting to offend, he tried to take another small sip from his cup. The drink didn't taste any better cold. He marveled that Fannie could sip the tea right down without a problem. He had to assume she drank the stuff so often she was immune to the taste.

She lifted an eyebrow before raising her cup to her lips, and then setting it down.

Gideon glanced at her cup, still as full as it had been when Lucy set it in front of her. He nailed her with a look of mock outrage.

She ducked her head. Her teacup rattled in the saucer.

Under his breath he said, "I defer to your masterful expertise. How do I get rid of this stuff?"

A smile flitted across her lips, before she said rather loudly, "It's late." She hesitated and looked at the clock on the wall. "Or very early, I should say. Aunt Lucy, Gideon is going to take his *Tay* with him."

Yep. No doubt about it. She was the master, getting rid of his tea *and* him.

"Morning will be here before you know it." Lucy whisked Gideon's cup away.

Susie rummaged in a cupboard and came up with a small thermos. "Pour the Tay in here, sister."

Rising from his chair, Gideon mouthed "thank you" to Fannie before walking over to the door. His shoes squished with each step.

Lucy pressed the thermos into his hand and said in a singsong voice, "Run between the raindrops."

Yeah. That isn't happening. The rain was coming down as hard, if not harder, than when he and Fannie came in. "Good night." With one last glance in Fannie's direction, he left.

Gideon entered the simple room, so different from the apartment he'd had before returning to Winsome. He shucked his suspenders and peeled off his shirt, vowing to get a raincoat the next time he went to town. It was the one item of clothing he'd forgotten to replace when he'd emptied his walk-in closet of English clothes. He now owned four sets of clothes, including his Sunday best, one felt hat, one straw hat, and the basics in footwear and toiletries.

Toeing out of his shoes, he padded barefoot to the window. He opened the sash wide enough to dump the horrid tea. From his vantage point, he could see the light in the kitchen.

Sitting in that cozy kitchen listening to Susie and Lucy talk to each other in Pennsylvania Dutch had brought back memories of sitting in his Mamm's kitchen and carrying on conversations in the dialect.

But there was a world of difference between Fannie's aunts and their chatter, and the boisterous exchanges Gideon had had with his two brothers. His Mamm and Daed often had to intervene and bring order to the dinner table.

Gideon closed his window and drew the shade. He'd overheard a bit of what Fannie's aunts had whispered to each other as they worked about the kitchen. They were plotting ways to make a match between Fannie and him. Had Fannie heard them?

They had to know he'd never been baptized into the church. He wasn't exactly husband material for a faithful Amish girl. Not yet, anyway.

3

In the early morning light, Gideon methodically worked his way back and forth across the land from the cut fence to the ditch, and from there to the edge of the road. Dew sparkled in the high grass, and bumblebees buzzed around a thick patch of clover.

Whoever cut the fence had left no clues in the tall weeds. The thought of Fannie coming to this lonely end of the pasture and meeting up with the person who had done this chilled him to the bone. Thankfully he'd gotten there ahead of her.

Giving up on finding anything that would help him figure out who had cut the fence, he pulled on the worn leather gloves he'd found in the shed.

He lifted a new piece of fencing into place and attached the wire to the part still standing. Pulling the wire taut, he reattached it to the fence post. To strengthen this section, he needed to pick up another post and one long piece of fencing when they went into town.

The incident left him uneasy. Who had done this? Fannie's idea that local teens were playing an innocent trick didn't sit right with him. *Rumspringa* for his crowd had meant driving fast cars and partying when not working the farm. They had never threatened friends' and neighbors' livelihoods.

If the local teens were not the culprits, there was another option that made him queasy. Fannie's aunts had given him a job and had welcomed him into their home. What if his return was the reason for this malicious act?

The squeak of the barn door and excited bleating of goats drifted across the tall grass of the pasture on a fresh morning breeze. Fannie had begun her chores. She'd be dressed properly this morning, unlike earlier when she'd had no time to twist her hair up or put on her prayer covering.

Gathering up the tools and loose pieces of fencing, Gideon walked back through the brush tangled with grapevines and sweet-smelling honeysuckle. He walked into the pasture. This piece of land would have proved hard to put to the plow. Outcroppings of rock rose from the tall grass here and there, creating the perfect playground for the goats.

Returning the tools and gloves to the shed, Gideon headed for the barn to see how far along Fannie was with the milking. He'd grown up around dairy cows, so the process wasn't completely foreign to him. Titus greeted him at the door of the barn.

"Hey, fella. Good job last night."

The big dog leaned against Gideon, as if begging for a rub behind his ears. Gideon complied as Fannie let the last doe into the milking parlor.

Last night they'd hurried through this room so fast, he hadn't had time to look around.

"Mornin', Fannie."

"Good morning." She turned away from him, a hint of pink touching her cheeks. Today, she wore a dark-brown dress. Her Kapp was securely in place. She reminded him of a busy little wren as she poured a ration of grain into the feeder for the nanny.

"You have a nice setup here." The room was spotless and well-appointed.

"Danke."

"What's her name?"

"What?" Fannie set aside the spray bottle of antibacterial cleaner she'd used to wash the doe's udder and settled beside her.

Gideon leaned against the doorframe. "I figure if I'm here to work with the goats, I should learn their names."

"Oh." Milk rang in the bottom of the stainless steel pail. "Tulip."

"Do they all have flower names?"

"Jah." She glanced at him, and then away. "Aunt Susie loves flowers."

Which accounted for all the flower beds in the yard and potted plants on the porch, but not Fannie's reserved manner. He tried to remember if he'd said anything last night to upset her. He'd respectfully turned his back so her aunt could doctor her knee. Did her skittishness have something to do with her aunts and their matchmaking efforts?

Wandering farther into the parlor, he glanced through the doorway into the milk room. The sight of the small strainer and pails swept him back in time to when he had helped with the cows on his family's farm. Something akin to homesickness settled in the pit of his stomach.

Rubbing his hand across his middle, he turned back to Fannie. "The fence is patched with a couple of short pieces."

"Danke."

"Should I let the nannies and kids outside now?" he asked.

She nodded, seeming to concentrate more than she needed to on the task at hand.

Though he was curious to know what was on her mind, he decided pushing her wouldn't help matters.

The does approached him when he walked into the loafing area. He slid the barn door open, and they streamed out into the warm sunshine. The kids followed, happy to be reunited with their mothers.

A short time after he fell into the rhythm of mucking out the barn, Tulip trotted past to join the herd. From the milk room came the sounds of stainless steel clinking and milk splashing. Fannie was cooling and processing the milk.

Gideon came back from dumping the wheelbarrow to find Fannie at the door wiping her hands on a cloth. "Breakfast should be ready." She ducked back into the parlor before he could respond.

This was just plain silly. They were going to be running into each other constantly throughout the day. He needed to know what he'd done to upset her. He followed her across the wet floor of the parlor and into the milk room.

"Have I done something wrong?"

The surprise in her eyes couldn't be faked. "No." Her hand went to her cheek and she turned away. "Help me carry the milk to the refrigerator in the washhouse, please." She reached for a handle, and he covered her hand with his.

Her breath caught, and her eyes grew round.

"Then what's going on?"

She dropped her hand and for the first time that morning looked him full in the face. "You left us, Gideon. I don't understand how you could do that." A frown pinched her eyebrows over the bridge of her pert nose.

Relieved to know her avoidance of him didn't have to do with a recent offense, Gideon picked up the pail and opened the door for her. She swept past him carrying a smaller one. "Rebellion. Pure and simple. Too many rules to live by." He had felt so restricted he thought he would die of suffocation. He wanted desperately to see and experience what the world held beyond the borders of Winsome.

"So why return? The rules haven't changed."

Gideon's pulse skipped. Leave it to Fannie to get to the heart of the matter. The question had no easy answer. He would give her the simple truth. "I experienced what the English world had to offer and decided I didn't like many of the values." He held the door into the washhouse for her.

She paused before entering, the golden flecks in her brown eyes sparkling in the sunlight. "It took you twelve years to figure that out?"

There wasn't a trace of sarcasm in her voice—only the desire to truly understand. He wasn't ready to tell her about Jacob's death. Gideon set the pails in the refrigerator.

"Guess I took longer than others to grow up." More than that, though, he'd never fully fit into the English society. He'd always felt like an outsider in that fast-paced world. "Please don't hold what I did twelve years ago against me."

Uncertainty flickered across her open, honest face. "That's hard to do."

He'd anticipated coming back would be difficult for many reasons. Winning Fannie Lapp's trust hadn't been on the list. But how she perceived him had rocketed to top priority in a few short hours. Forgiving others was the Amish way. On the other hand, he was asking her to forgive him before she fully knew and understood the depth of forgiveness he needed.

After they'd washed up, he walked with her along the path that led to the kitchen door. In the flower beds on either side, the showy bearded irises were past their prime, but the daylilies were bursting with orange and yellow life. The tantalizing smell of frying bacon wafted out the open kitchen window.

His stomach growled.

A smile played across Fannie's lips. "I think it's time to eat." She climbed up the steps and went indoors before he realized she'd never said she would forgive him.

"There you are." Lucy patted a kitchen chair and motioned for Gideon to sit. Fannie had slipped into the seat across the table.

In the center of the table, the fat on the bacon sizzled. Steam rose from a pan of golden sticky buns. A bowl of scrambled eggs sat beside a dish filled with hash browns.

His mouth watering, Gideon bowed his head, hoping Susie didn't make silent table grace last forever. Thankfully, that prayer was answered when she picked up her fork with a clink.

Lucy held a spoon over the eggs. "Pass me your plate." After loading his dish with eggs, she moved on to the potatoes. "You're too skinny. A man alone in the city doesn't eat right. Restaurants serve two mouthfuls of food and call it a meal. Good home-cooked food will fatten you up." Taking up tongs, she added strips of bacon. One promptly slid off the plate.

"He's not a steer going to market, sister." Susie picked up the bacon strip and matter-of-factly plopped it back on top of his eggs as though rescuing fallen food was a regular occurrence. "Be sure he gets a bun. I made them fresh this morning."

In the midst of their chatter, Gideon heard a soft strangled sound. He glanced across the table at Fannie.

She had her napkin up to her face covering her mouth. The corners of her eyes crinkled, giving away her effort not to laugh.

And just like that, hearing her laugh before the meal ended became his goal.

Fighting to keep his face serious, he narrowed his eyes in mock anger.

Her eyes widened. Her gaze fell to his lips as he struggled not to smile.

Fannie pressed her napkin hard against her mouth. If she didn't giggle, she would choke for sure.

Last night's decision to keep Gideon at a distance was evaporating with the steam rising from the breakfast table. The man disturbed her to the point of killing her appetite.

"Fannie, hold up your plate."

"Only a little please, *Tantchen*."

"Jah." Aunt Lucy dug deep into the eggs and placed a mound on Fannie's plate rivaling the pile in front of Gideon.

Fannie's stomach curled in protest.

Switching to the tongs, Aunt Lucy waved them over the bacon. "You need to keep up your strength."

"Only two slices of bacon, please."

"Are you sick?" Aunt Susie bounced out of her chair. Her hand went to Fannie's brow and then was followed by her lips pressed against the same spot.

Fannie tried to dodge the hand and lips but failed. "Nee. I'm not sick." From beneath Aunt Susie's sagging chin, she made a face at Gideon. Two could play his game.

Gideon crossed his eyes at her before digging into his hash browns.

"You aren't hot enough to sting my lips." Aunt Susie sat in her chair.

"If you're not sick, what's wrong?" Waving the tongs which were holding a slice of crisp bacon through the air, Aunt Lucy leaned forward. "Do you need a tonic?"

"Nee!" Panic raced through Fannie. Aunt Lucy's remedies tasted like death.

Gideon coughed hard, clearly trying to hide his laughter.

Aunt Susie bounced up yet again and thumped his back between his shoulder blades.

His eyes watered. Fannie wasn't sure whether the tears were from the effort to breathe or not laugh.

Meeting Aunt Lucy's questioning gaze, Fannie said, "Keeping up my strength isn't a worry." She'd always been healthy, but Aunt Lucy had taken a notion and needed to be convinced. "I'm not doing the hard labor now. Gideon does it."

Around the table, all motion ceased, as though someone had yanked on a wagon brake. Mouths agape, the sisters stared at each other. A look passed between them and Aunt Lucy lowered the tongs.

Fannie's heart sank. She'd seen that look before, and it did not bode well.

Nonchalantly, Aunt Lucy served her sister. "It's nice to have a strong man to help, jah?"

"Jah. Many hands make light work." Aunt Susie smiled at Gideon.

"And the work gets done faster." Aunt Lucy took a sticky bun.

Gideon looked at Fannie and raised his eyebrows in question.

Fannie shook her head at him before holding out her plate. "May I have a sticky bun, please?"

Aunt Susie frowned. "Are you sure you should have one?"

"I'm feeling fine." And she loved sticky buns.

"Of course you are."

Oh dear. What was going on behind those faded gray eyes?

"I'd like more than a pile of scrambled eggs for breakfast."

"Well, if you insist." Aunt Susie selected the smallest bun in the pan and placed it on Fannie's plate.

Fannie took a bite, relishing the yeasty goodness fragrant with cinnamon and glazed with icing. "Before we can make more soap, I need to go into town for lye."

"I should pick up more fencing. I'll drive you." Gideon forked fluffy yellow eggs into his mouth.

Smiles fluttered back and forth between the aunts.

"I'll make sandwiches from yesterday's chicken." Aunt Susie smiled broadly. "You can stop for a picnic beside the river. Fannie, you know the place."

The bite of sticky bun turned to chalk in Fannie's mouth. Yes, she knew the place. It was a lovely spot beneath an ancient maple tree. Easily seen from the road, it was public yet at the same time private. The spot was favored by courting couples.

"That's a splendid idea." Aunt Lucy clapped her hands together. "I'll open the last jar of the banana pickles." She patted Gideon's arm. "Last year we had a bumper crop of cucumbers."

"We'll pack the lunch while you go wash and change, Fannie." Aunt Susie rose and began assembling sandwiches, her plate of food barely touched.

Aunt Lucy headed for the basement stairs to raid the shelves of home-preserved food.

Fannie stared solemnly at Gideon. He was busy finishing up the last of his eggs and hash browns. Did he remember that place on the river? The shade of the tree had been a favorite spot among couples for generations. Someone had named it the Courting Tree.

Popping the last bite of sticky bun into his mouth, he finally looked at her. His eyes held a warm glint that sent heat rushing to her cheeks. He winked, and she lifted her hand to cover her scar.

Afraid he was being railroaded by her aunts, Fannie blurted, "Are you sure you want to go to town?"

He frowned. "Yes. Why do you ask?"

"Well, I could always pick up the fence for you if you have other things to do."

He hesitated, giving Aunt Susie time to dive into the conversation.

"Gideon works for us. If he needs fencing and supplies, he should go after them to make sure he gets exactly what he needs."

Her meager attempt to give him a way out thwarted, Fannie started to clear the table.

"Leave that for us, Fannie. Go change into something besides that chore dress. You're going to town." Aunt Lucy plunked a jar of banana pickles on the counter and made shooing motions with her hands.

Wiping his mouth with his napkin, Gideon stood. "What can I do to help?"

Fannie pointed to the door. "The small pail of milk in the milking parlor is for Sarah's son Malachi. Will you go get it so we can drop it off?"

Nodding, he ducked out of the kitchen and headed for the washhouse.

Her aunts stood side by side at the counter chattering in Pennsylvania Dutch, hoping out loud that the picnic they prepared would advance Fannie's chances of landing a husband.

Mortified by their conversation, Fannie hurried up the stairs to change.

Walking the lane that connected the Grossdawdi Haus and the big house was always a treat for Fannie. The sun warmed the earth, filling the air with the mellow fragrance of ripening crops. On one side of the lane, the soft green of the alfalfa waved in a gentle breeze. On the other side, dairy cows lolled beneath the pasture oak, flicking their tails at flies and chewing their cuds.

Fannie took a deep breath. The usually peaceful walk filled her with anxiety today. She looked down at her shoes. Each step she took sent a puff of dust into the air. "I need to apologize for my aunts." The basket holding their lunch banged against the side of her leg with each step. "I don't know what got into them, acting like this trip into town was something more than just a plain old trip into town."

Gideon's silence unnerved her. After what felt like forever, she glanced sidelong at him.

He stared off into the distance, seeming to consider what she had said.

"I'm sorry, Gideon." Her voice came out a hoarse whisper, nearly lost in the raucous squabbling of two crows wheeling low across the sky.

"You have nothing to apologize for, Fannie." He looked at her and shrugged. "It's the way of life here. I'd forgotten how the hopes of the older generation are wrapped up in seeing the next generation continue this way of life."

Fannie's heart dropped with agonizing swiftness. Stated in such a matter-of-fact tone, his critique created a cold knot of disappointment in her stomach. Mentally chiding herself for hoping for something different, she picked up the pace. Hadn't she decided yesterday she wouldn't trust him fully?

"I've been thinking about last night," Gideon admitted.

Fannie's fingers played across her scar. Which part of last night? She didn't dare ask, knowing he would tell her soon enough.

"While we're in town, I'll go to the sheriff's office and report what happened."

Shock jolted through Fannie. She stopped in her tracks. "Nee!"

He jerked to a stop, causing the lid on the milk pail to rattle. "Why not?"

She shook her head. "It was a prank by youngsters. That's all. I'll warn the neighbors to watch their livestock."

"I can make the fence stronger, and I will, but that won't stop someone from cutting the wires again."

He sounded like an adult speaking to a child, which heightened her anger. It was all she could do not to stamp her foot like the youngster he seemed to think she was.

"The authorities need to be told, Fannie."

She walked at a faster pace, which emphasized her limp. "That is the English way, not ours. You admit you've forgotten how strongly the elders focus on the next generation following in their footsteps. I think you have forgotten a great deal more." Sadness hung about her like the heavy wool cloak she wore in the winter. She was becoming more convinced with each passing hour that he would not be able to transition back into their way of life. It would only be a matter of time before he realized it too.

"The goats returned unharmed this time. There is no guarantee they will be so lucky the next time." The glint of conviction sparked in his eyes. "It would be a terrible loss for your aunts and their business."

Sadness weighed on Fannie's heart. The terrible loss would be if he got baptized and then decided to leave the settlement again. He would be under the *Bann*.

4

By the time they arrived at the back door of the main house, three guinea hens, two dogs, and a child had announced their presence. Seven-year-old Micah raced indoors to tell his mother that Fannie had arrived and that she had a man with her.

Sarah appeared in the doorway with two-year-old Malachi on her hip. She was one of the lucky few that appeared radiant during pregnancy. "*Wilkum*, Fannie." She looked at Gideon and recognition flickered across her face. "It's been a long time, Gideon."

Gideon's response was cool. "Hello, Sarah."

Wondering about his reserved manner, Fannie pointed to the pail he held. "We brought fresh milk for Malachi."

"Danke." Sarah stepped back allowing Fannie and Gideon to enter.

He went to the refrigerator and set the pail inside.

Fannie dragged her gaze away from him only to find Sarah watching her closely. "May we take the buggy into town? I need lye, and Gideon wants to pick up a roll of fence."

"Of course." Sarah shifted Malachi into a more comfortable position. "Samuel is in the barn. He'll show Gideon which horse and tack to use."

"Danke." Fannie turned to follow Gideon, but she was stopped by Sarah's hand on her arm.

"Gideon will let us know when he's ready to leave. Come see what I'm making for the baby." Sarah led Fannie into the small front parlor. The room lay in shadows, untouched by the morning sun. A sewing basket overflowed next to one of the cushioned chairs.

Sarah set Malachi on the rag rug and fussed with him until the kitchen door closed behind Gideon. Rising, she plunked both hands on her hips and exclaimed, "Gideon Zook? *He's* the man Mamm hired to help with the goats?" She put her hand to her forehead as if fighting off an impending headache and narrowed her eyes. "Did she *know* who she was hiring?"

Fannie nodded and splayed her fingers across the scar on her cheek.

Spying the picnic basket in Fannie's other hand, disbelief etched Sarah's features into sharp relief. She spun around to look out the open window. The ties of her Kapp trailed down her back. Hands fisted at her sides, she took deep breaths before turning back to face Fannie.

Fannie took a step back.

"He was the wildest of the boys in my crowd, Fannie." Her expression taut, Sarah lifted her chin. "He cannot be trusted. He's schooled in the ways of the English. He would think nothing of taking advantage of you. Or Mamm and Aunt Lucy, for that matter."

Having her thoughts echoed by Sarah was disconcerting and a little frightening. Fannie shifted the picnic basket to her other hand. "I'll be careful."

Taking Fannie's free hand, Sarah sank into one of the chairs by the window and pulled Fannie down beside her. "My Rumspringa was very different from yours. Where you enjoyed going to the movies on occasion, I took full advantage of the freedom and did a great deal more." Sarah shook her head, her voice wistful.

Fannie set the picnic basket on the floor. Sarah spoke the truth. She had been out of control during those years. Aunt Susie and Uncle Will had been terribly worried about her.

Fannie didn't have an adventurous bone in her body. Unrestrained partying wasn't in her makeup. Fading into the background suited her fine. She'd never been so happy as she was the day she decided she was finished with the whole thing. She was happiest at home helping Uncle Will and Aunt Susie. "You stayed. You were baptized into the church."

"I almost didn't stay."

Sarah's words ricocheted through Fannie with sharp percussion. She sat back, pulling her hand from Sarah's grip. "You questioned joining the church?"

"Yes." A light breeze came through the window, capturing a single golden hair that had escaped Sarah's morning grooming. "There is so much out there, Fannie. So much we can never experience again." Bitterness edged her cousin's voice. "Sometimes I wish I had done what you did and ignored the whole tradition. Then I would never have known what I walked away from."

Fannie's heart skipped a beat. "There is much that is not good about the English way of life too, Sarah. Don't look at only one side." Fannie's mind careened between what she thought she knew about Sarah and the truth. "There's is so much to love here." Fannie gathered Malachi into her arms. Sarah was blessed with so much. How could she question the decision she'd made all those years ago?

Sarah stared out the window with her mouth set in a firm line.

"You stayed with us, Sarah. You made the right choice."

"Did I?" Sarah rose from the chair. Her hand went to her lower back in an effort to relieve the ache from carrying the baby's extra weight. "Sometimes I wonder, Fannie."

Fannie set Malachi down and reached for the picnic basket. Sarah had the life Fannie prayed to have. A loving husband, adorable children, and a home of her own. What had she turned her back on that could compare with any of that?

"Fannie?" Gideon's voice traveled through the house. "The buggy is ready."

"I'll be out in a moment." Fannie rose from the chair. She needed time to consider all Sarah had revealed. "The youngsters are pulling pranks that are not funny. Someone cut the fence last night and three goats got out. Tell Samuel to watch his fences and cows. No telling what they will do next." She kissed Sarah's smooth cheek and let herself out the kitchen door.

Her heart heavy, Fannie walked across the gravel drive to where the horse, Kelly, was hitched to a rail. Accepting Gideon's helping hand, she climbed into the buggy and set the picnic basket in the back.

Samuel gave Gideon a few last-minute tips about this particular horse and her quirks.

Gideon settled onto the seat, and the buggy rocked beneath his weight. Lifting the reins, he clucked his tongue. "I haven't harnessed a horse in years. I fumbled a few times, but I haven't forgotten how to do it."

"That's *gut*." Engrossed in her thoughts about the conversation with Sarah, Fannie stared straight ahead.

If Gideon joined the church, would his happiness turn bitter? Would he live with his regrets or would he once again leave the community—this time under the Bann?

Sarah had warned her about Gideon. Her head understood the danger. Now if only her heart would listen.

Gideon relaxed into the task of driving. The familiar sway of the buggy and the sound of Kelly's hooves against the asphalt road sent a wave of nostalgia crashing through him. He hadn't realized how much he missed riding in a buggy. Thankfully, the skills he had learned early in life remained a part of him.

He glanced at Fannie sitting quietly at his side. How much did she know about Sarah's running-around years? He'd never courted her, but Sarah had been foolhardy like him.

Gideon became wrapped up in his own thoughts and watching traffic. They were almost to town before he realized Fannie hadn't said a word.

A heavy scowl creased her brow.

"A penny for them."

"What?" Her eyes clouded with confusion as though he'd pulled her back from a long way away.

"You're deep in thought. I just offered you money if you shared what you were thinking."

She gave an unladylike snort and waved her hand at him. "A poor investment of your pennies. Better to keep them."

"Says you." He missed the teasing camaraderie they'd had over breakfast when her aunts had set their mind to matchmaking. He didn't worry about himself, but Fannie might be uncomfortable, and that *did* bother him.

The traffic grew heavier as they approached town. Samuel had made a point of choosing Kelly for Gideon to drive. She was a steady animal and exactly what he needed to get used to the mix of horse and automobile traffic on the busy streets of town.

"Are we going to Willard's Hardware?" He'd been gone long enough that the store could have closed.

"Yes. It's still the only hardware store in town."

After arriving at their destination, Gideon reined Kelly in at the hitching rail and climbed down from the buggy.

An Amish man stepped out of the store and onto the street. Dressed like all the other men in the settlement, there was something about this man's walk . . . A mix of surprise and joy swept through Gideon. The man was his brother.

Abram looked up and came to a halt as his eyes focused on Gideon.

Gideon's heart jackhammered. His younger brother was no longer a clean-shaven youth. He wore the beard of a married man. The shock of that revelation hit Gideon like a blow to the midsection. His brother had married, and he had missed the wedding.

Looking each other in the eye seemed to go on forever before Abram turned his back on Gideon and walked up the street toward the feed store.

A cold knot formed in the pit of his stomach as Gideon held out his hand to help Fannie down.

She didn't budge. Instead, she looked from him to the retreating back of his brother, then back at him. "You should follow him and say hello."

"If he wanted to speak to me, he would have." Gideon fought the sick feeling in his gut.

"Perhaps he's thinking the same thing about you."

Gideon gritted his teeth. "A confrontation on Main Street is not the way I want to renew relationships with my family." Though he didn't think for a minute Abram would be confrontational. No, he'd always do what all good Amish men do. He'd turn away, like he had this time.

Disappointment shadowed Fannie's face. Her gaze followed Abram. "I don't understand either of you. I would do whatever it took to speak to my Mamm and Daed if they were on this earth."

Her words skewered him. He dropped his hand to his side, feeling like an insensitive clod. Walking back around the buggy, he climbed in and took his seat at her side.

"What are you doing?" She looked at him askance.

He shifted so he was facing her. "Apologizing to you."

"For what?"

"For not having the slightest inkling what my family drama would look like from your perspective." He was uncomfortable under her direct gaze, but he didn't look away. "I have a hope of reconnecting with my family that you don't have."

"That hope could be snatched away from you at any moment, Gideon." Her voice carried a sad note.

"You're right." He wanted to pull her close but to do so would shock her, so instead he took her hand. The gesture was met with a gasp, but he didn't let go. "I can't imagine going through what happened to you." He rubbed the bridge of his nose. "I was just a kid when the accident happened, but I don't think I ever talked to you about it."

She shrugged. "You could have and I wouldn't remember."

"What do you remember?"

"Bits and pieces. I was five years old and suddenly thrust into the strange world of the English hospital."

Fannie's eyes seemed to stare through him, causing the back of Gideon's neck to prickle.

"What I remember most was wanting my Mamm and Daed." She took a shaky breath. "Aunt Susie and Uncle Will were wonderful, but they weren't my parents."

Gideon squeezed her hand bringing her back to the present.

Her gaze cleared and her eyes focused on him. "For years after, I was afraid to ride in a buggy."

In an effort to lighten the mood, he looked at her in mock horror. "And you let me drive the buggy today?"

She chuckled. "I was watching traffic and ready to intervene at any moment."

Gideon slapped his free hand to his chest. "You wound my pride, woman."

Fannie rolled her eyes. "Good. Pride is a sin." She tightened her hand around his and her expression became serious. "Danke for asking, Gideon."

It was his turn to be serious. "I notice sometimes your limp is worse."

She nodded. "If I overdo, my hip bothers me."

An understatement he was sure. "Then we'll have to be careful. I clean the barn now, so no more pushing wheelbarrows."

Her hand jerked in his, but he held on, not letting her cover her scar. "You know what I think, Fannie Lapp?"

"No, but I think you're about to tell me." A tiny grin tipped her lips.

"I think you are courageous."

Her gaze dropped to their linked hands, and her cheeks turned a pretty pink. She whispered, "Danke." She shifted in the seat and looked up at him. "I think it's time to get our shopping done, jah?"

Gideon gave her hand one last squeeze before letting go and jumping from the buggy. This time she accepted his help climbing out. Cupping her elbow in his hand, he walked at her side on the sidewalk in front of the store.

An English family had stopped across the street, staring and snapping pictures. Feeling protective, he placed himself between them and Fannie, doing his best to shield her from their unwitting intrusion and lack of respect. To his chagrin, she noticed.

"They're taking pictures of you too, you know. Not just me and the horse."

"I don't care if they take my picture."

She sighed. "You should, or have you forgotten photographs are considered graven images?"

"I haven't forgotten." He didn't care a whit about having his picture taken. His concern was her discomfort with the situation. Opening the door for her, he followed her inside the store.

The mix of smells unique to an old hardware store carried him back through a time warp. The tang of leather, the metallic smell of oiled tools, and the sharp chemical smell of fertilizer enveloped him.

Fannie touched his arm. She had a worried frown on her face. "Are you all right?"

He shook his head, feeling dazed. "It hasn't changed." He felt like he'd stepped back in time.

"But you have."

The steady gaze of her brown eyes dug into him. The sadness in her voice brought him up short. How could he explain the emotions rolling through him? Aisle three was not the place for this conversation. "I'll go get the fencing." Disconcerted by her observation, he left her standing there.

With a roll of wire balanced on his shoulder and a new metal post in hand, Gideon headed toward the front of the store, where he found Fannie holding a plastic container of lye and talking to a friend. When he approached, she introduced Rachel Stoltzfus.

He didn't remember Rachel, but that didn't mean she wouldn't remember him. Uncertain of his welcome, he was relieved when the woman seemed genuinely pleased to meet him.

When she learned his parents were Daniel and Katie Zook, her wide round face lit up. "I'm glad your Daed is feeling better. He didn't take kindly to being laid up, that one. My husband, John, was to help Abram with the farm and the carpentry in the meantime."

Gideon's stomach churned sour. His father had been ill, and he hadn't known. His brother had needed help on the farm, and he hadn't been there to lend a hand. He was trying to form a question that didn't reveal the extent of his ignorance when Fannie cut into the other woman's chatter.

"I told Rachel what happened last night. She has two goats and a small flock of sheep." Fannie rushed through her explanation, barely taking a breath. "She and John will be on the lookout for anything suspicious."

In the matter of a minute, Fannie and Rachel were saying their goodbyes, and Fannie was checking out. Gideon followed Fannie's lead, but couldn't stop thinking about his family. They'd experienced hardship, and he'd been oblivious the entire time.

After helping Fannie into the buggy, he untied Kelly and took his seat. He sat unmoving until Fannie looked at him. "What happened to my father?"

Her hand on her cheek, Fannie studied Kelly like this was her first time seeing the tail end of a horse. "He broke his arm is all."

Is all. For a man whose physical labor provided for his family, a broken anything would mean being unable to work at full capacity.

"How?" He felt small having to ask.

"He took a misstep and fell off a ladder." Her hand remained over her scar.

"What was he building?"

"Abram has set up a woodworking shop. They make gazebos and the matching garden furniture to go in them."

The magnitude of all he'd missed pressed in on Gideon. Over the last few years, he'd eased his conscience with the knowledge that tradition held change in the settlement to a snail's pace. He'd convinced himself there was little he would miss. He had time.

Then his friend Jacob had died, and here Gideon was discovering what a fool he'd been.

Was Abram's attitude a reflection of his parents' feelings toward him? Had he been overconfident when he'd told Fannie he had a hope she no longer had? Daed was a minister in the church. Because of his position, the community held him and his family to a higher standard. To find his way back into the community and the church, Gideon would need to speak with the bishop.

Fannie dropped her hand from her face and knotted her fingers together in her lap. "I feel bad you had to hear about your family from a stranger." She huffed. "I let Rachel Stoltzfus give you the news instead of telling you myself. I should have." Her voice dropped to a whisper. "I thought you knew."

The warmth in her brown eyes loosened the hard knot of self-condemnation in his chest. "Thank you."

"For what?"

"Caring. Do you know what else is happening with my family?"

She settled more comfortably on the seat. "Your parents are visiting Joshua in Indiana."

Gideon took up the reins. Why hadn't Leland mentioned that? Perhaps he thought Gideon would use it as an excuse to delay his homecoming. By now Joshua and Christine would have children of their own, something Gideon had known would happen someday, but hadn't thought a great deal about until he realized someday was here. He had either nieces or nephews—maybe both—that he'd never met. They had an uncle who didn't know their names.

With a gentle pull on the lines and low voice commands, he backed Kelly away from the rail. Concentrating on the traffic, he urged her to enter the driving lane, and they were on their way. He waited until they reached the quiet edges of town before speaking again. "Where do you want to stop to eat the lunch your aunts packed?"

"Not at the Courting Tree."

Her answer was so immediate, he couldn't keep the smile off his face. "Agreed."

"There are picnic tables at the baseball field. We can stop there."

"Sounds good to me." He'd spent many a summer evening playing ball in that field.

When they arrived, the baseball field was empty, but the small playground teemed with activity. English mothers and a couple of fathers chatted while their children ran between the slide, monkey bars, and swings.

Finding a table away from the hubbub, Fannie spread a cloth and proceeded to set out sandwiches made from thick slices of homemade bread and stuffed with chicken salad. She quickly filled the table with Lucy's banana pickles, deviled eggs, fruit salad, chocolate cupcakes, and iced tea.

Gideon stared at the amount of food in awe. "How many people did they think they were feeding?" After the mixed emotions accompanying his step back in time, being snubbed by his brother, and discovering his father had been injured, Fannie's quiet chuckle was a balm to Gideon's heart.

"Feeding people is how they show love." A bright shade of pink bloomed across her cheeks. "I guess it's how they show their gratitude too."

Gideon took a huge bite from his sandwich instead of acknowledging what she'd said about love. He hadn't worked for her aunts long enough for them to consider him part of the family. He was more than happy to settle on gratitude as their motive. "They're good cooks."

"They are." She fussed with her fruit salad before adding with a shade of shyness, "I made the bread."

"You're an excellent baker." He took another appreciative bite of his sandwich. Pleased that she was talking to him about something other than the goats and fencing, he dared to ask her a question. "Your aunts appear able to care for themselves. How did you end up living in the Grossdawdi Haus with them?"

Her head jerked up, and she stared at him wide-eyed. "You have a way of asking the most personal questions, Gideon."

He popped half of a deviled egg in his mouth, chewed, and swallowed. He knew that. What he didn't know was if she would answer his question. "I love deviled eggs. Haven't eaten one in years." He finished his sandwich and was eyeing the cupcakes when she spoke.

"Sarah's husband, Samuel, is a middle brother of ten. It was only practical that he take over the farm." She brushed imaginary crumbs from the tablecloth. "Aunt Lucy has lived with us for years. When she and Aunt Susie moved to the little house, it was logical for me to go too."

There was something she wasn't saying. He tried to imagine what he would feel like being the extra in a home inhabited by newlyweds. "You felt unwelcome with Sarah and Samuel?"

"Nee!" She turned to look at the children on the swings. Their mothers pushed them higher and higher, and their laughter turned to squeals.

Gideon didn't take his gaze off her, willing her to give him the full answer.

Her shoulders slumped. She crumpled her paper napkin tight in her fist. "I couldn't stay and watch Sarah have the family I've always dreamed of having."

Of course. He was a complete and utter fool. Taking a cupcake from the plastic container, he berated himself for his own idiocy. Fannie had been brought up to want one thing and one thing only. A family of her own. Such training ensured the continuation of the community.

"I should have realized that. I'm sorry." How could he prove to her that he was capable of returning to the community when forgetting the simplest doctrines caused him to stick his foot in his mouth?

He contemplated the cupcakes. Even though he was stuffed to the gills, he couldn't resist taking another one. Hopefully eating it would keep him from chewing on shoe leather again.

Fannie nudged the container closer to him, a wisp of a smile on her lips. "I think you've forgotten a great deal about us, Gideon. Are you sure you can return?"

5

Fannie pressed the lid on the small plastic tub and placed it on the kitchen counter next to the others ready to go to the freezer. Gideon stood at her side measuring milk. She tried not to think about the warmth radiating from him. She tried not to let his clean male scent distract her. But worst of all, she had to control the impulse to touch his hair and smooth the cowlick usually hidden beneath his hat.

He slid the next tub of milk in her direction.

Her fingers brushed his hand, sending a jolt of awareness zinging through her. She glanced at him, and her heart stuttered. Captured in the warmth of his smile, she smiled back. He'd been adamant about helping her measure the goats' milk into containers for the freezer. She considered packaging the milk women's work. He considered it a learning experience.

"That's the last of it."

Fannie blinked. "What?"

He pointed at the tub in front of her. "That's all the milk." He set the pail in the sink with a clang.

"Oh." Her fingers fumbled with the lid. "That's *gut.*" *You sound like a ninny, Fannie.* Trying to cover her embarrassment, she said the first thing that popped into her head. "The milk has to be frozen to make soap."

His brow crinkled in a frown. "Why?"

"The chemical reaction. The lye can make the milk so hot that the milk will burn if it isn't cold enough." Her heart flip-flopped over the smile playing across his lips.

"I guess frozen is as cold as it gets."

Fannie nodded. "We rent a freezer from Leland James. The little hand wagon I use to carry the milk there is in the shed."

"I'll get it." Gideon left, taking his hat from the peg by the door.

Through the window, Fannie watched him walk across the yard. Her heart had done nothing but quiver the entire time they had worked together. It would become fatigued if she didn't get herself under control. She was supposed to be watching for trouble, not watching for opportunities to know him better.

Marking each tub with the date, she placed them in a cardboard box. Sarah's words of warning were challenged by the pleasure of working with Gideon. Always cautious, Fannie had never before experienced the delight that fizzed through her when she was with Gideon. If this was what falling in love felt like, she now understood the allure.

Shaking her head, she marked the next tub. *What silliness.* She was setting herself up for disappointment. When he decided he couldn't live plain, no matter how much he wanted to change, life on the farm would once again be humdrum. She thumped the tub in the box. For today, a little bit of happiness was a fine thing. "But don't get used to it, Fannie."

"Get used to what?" Gideon walked into the room.

Fannie jumped, causing the marker to fly from her hand. Horrified, she stared at him.

He picked the marker up off the floor and handed it back to her. "Get used to what?"

"Um. Ah." She had never been good at lying. "Your help."

His eyes narrowed slightly before taking the carton and walking out to the wagon.

Thankful he didn't pursue the matter, Fannie gathered together the meal Aunt Susie had made for the Jameses. Setting it in her basket, she followed him out.

He placed the cardboard box in the wooden wagon Uncle Will had built for her when she'd first come to live with him and Aunt Susie. Gideon picked up the handle suited to the height of an adult. "Did your uncle replace the original handle?"

"Yes. As I grew, the length of the handle grew with me." She fell into step beside him.

"Making do and using what you have." He murmured the words thoughtfully.

"It's our way of life."

"Last week I would have loaded the milk in a car and driven over to Leland's." He paused. "Actually, I would have had my own freezer and not needed to drive this anywhere."

Apprehension settled in Fannie's chest. She did her best to ignore it, instead choosing to admire the beauty around her.

Overhead, puffy, white clouds broke the expanse of vivid blue sky. Light glinted off the shiny black feathers of the crows circling Leland's cornfield. A gentle breeze swished across the emerald field, rattling the wide leaves inhabited by chirping crickets.

Too soon, the lane ended and they were at the home of Leland and Prudy James. In one corner of the yard near the driveway, a cinder-block building with a grapevine wreath on the door gleamed white in the sunshine.

Using the key she had attached to her wrist with a curly pink cord, Fannie unlocked the door. She held it open for Gideon, and he carried the carton inside. "Our freezer is the one on the far end."

The room held five freezers. Each one belonged to a different Amish family in the area. A desk and chair were positioned against one wall. A black telephone, a pad of paper, and a canning jar filled with pens and pencils were on the desk. On the wall over the desk, a corkboard held the hardware store calendar, business cards, and a phone list.

Setting the carton on the floor in front of the freezer Fannie indicated, Gideon left her to the business of storing the milk and wandered over to the desk.

Troubled, Fannie surreptitiously watched him while she worked. He was being confronted with another aspect of her life. The life he'd left.

As though feeling her gaze upon him, he glanced over his shoulder. "This is nicer than the phone shack I used growing up." He pointed to the list. "Drivers?"

"Yes." Telephones in the house and cars to drive long distances were two things Gideon had become accustomed to while living like the English. A knot formed in the pit of Fannie's stomach.

He leaned in closer to the list. "I recognize a few of the names." He took his hat off, wiped his brow with his forearm, and jammed his hat back on. "Living simple takes a lot of work."

"Hard work isn't a bad thing." Fannie picked up the box and stepped closer. "It's a *gut* way to live." She was surprised by how important it had become to convince him of that. "When was the last time you walked between cornfields, or stopped and listened to the birds sing?"

His mouth tilted into the heart-stopping smile Fannie remembered from long ago. "You have me there." He tipped his head thoughtfully.

Was he counting the years?

"Not since I left Winsome," he said finally. "And I enjoyed the walk. Especially because I got to take that walk with you."

Oh my. Her breath hitched. Not wanting to give her wayward heart more encouragement, Fannie whisked passed him and out the door. "I have a meal to deliver to the house."

Leland's welcome was warm. She asked, "How is Prudy today?"

Leland ran a hand over his iron-gray hair. "It's a good day. She's in her chair out back."

After placing the meal in the refrigerator, Fannie followed the men to the back patio.

Prudy sat in her wheelchair reading a book. The short gray curls framing her face held a sparkly little barrette.

Fannie took the seat next to her. "I brought Aunt Susie's chicken and dumplings for your dinner tonight."

"Thank you, and please thank your aunt for me." Crippling rheumatoid arthritis limited Prudy's ability to move about and keep her home as she had in the past. The disease had robbed her of many things, but she hadn't let the challenges dampen her outlook on life. "Isn't today glorious?" She lifted her face to the sun, enjoying the warmth on her skin.

In her seventies, Prudy faithfully applied lipstick and rouge as part of her morning routine. On one visit, she had explained to Fannie applying makeup was one of the few things she could still do for herself, and "having her face on" lifted her spirits.

While the men discussed buggies and horses for sale at an upcoming auction, Fannie entertained Prudy with the latest escapades of Sarah's children. Soon the time came to leave.

Fannie placed a tiny plastic container in Prudy's misshapen hand. "I made a lotion using our milk and essential oils. I hope it eases some of your pain."

"Thank you." Placing crooked fingers on Fannie's arm, she patted it and whispered, "Gideon is a nice young man."

Heat spread up Fannie's neck and across her cheeks. "Jah."

Prudy chuckled. "You folks don't talk about romance, but it does exist. Look at my Leland. He takes good care of me. He picked out my barrette this morning."

Fannie's astonishment must have shown because Prudy chuckled. "I know. Each of his hands is the size of a five-pound ham, but he's gentle when he cares for me." Moisture gathered in her eyes. "I don't know what I would do without him. Truly I don't."

"I'm sure he feels the same way about you." Fannie held her friend's hand, absorbing the feel of the knotted knuckles and crooked fingers.

"We met late in life." Prudy blinked hard. "Did you know that?" Fannie shook her head.

"That's why we don't have any children." She squeezed Fannie's hand. "But we have each other. And that isn't simply enough—it's everything." She paused for a moment, her clear hazel eyes drifting across Fannie's face. "I know how deeply you desire a family, Fannie, because I was once young like you. Not Amish, of course, but that yearning is something any woman can experience. Love will come to you. Not necessarily the way you hoped for or expected, but don't rule out what God has planned for you and the man you will love. Be open for God to fulfill your dream in a way you don't expect."

Fannie's response stuck in the back of her throat, wrapped around a sob that would escape if she said so much as a word.

"It's time for you to rest in bed, Prudy." Leland approached with concern in his eyes.

"You're a good husband, Leland. Have I told you that?" She smiled up at him, love radiating from her face.

"Several times a day. You make it easy to be good to you." He leaned down and kissed his wife.

Fannie hurried to rise. Beautiful as the sentiments were, she didn't understand how Leland and Prudy could act so intimately in front of her and Gideon. "It's been wonderful visiting with you. Bye now."

"Do come again soon, Fannie. And Gideon."

"We will." Leading Gideon off the patio and around to the front of the house, Fannie hurried as fast as her hip would allow across the yard to the lane between the cornfields. Gideon walked behind her.

The empty wagon rattled and bumped across the yard.

His hand closed about her elbow. "Where's the fire?"

She glanced over her shoulder at him. "There is no fire. I didn't want to overstay our welcome." She didn't allow herself to get caught in his gaze. She didn't want him to see her discomfort.

His hand dropped away, but he kept pace with her. "Did I do or say something wrong in front of the Jameses?"

Surprise speared through Fannie. "Nee!" She shook her head. "They are Englischers." She wanted to say *like you*, but caught herself before the words came out of her mouth.

"Then why the abrupt departure?"

Considering his question, she slowed her pace. Sarah's words flashed through Fannie's mind.

He's schooled in the ways of the English now.

Here was another difference between them she could point out. "I was uncomfortable."

"With what?"

"Their . . . display of affection."

He looked at her, puzzled. "What display of affection?"

Fannie looked at him in disbelief. "Sharing their feelings for each other and then kissing in front of us."

Halting in his tracks, Gideon stared at her. "You mean when she said he was a good husband and he gave her a kiss?"

Looking at the toes of her shoes, she nodded. "There is no need to say those things or kiss in front of company."

Gideon was quiet for what seemed an eternity before he spoke. "That's the Amish way."

She released a breath she hadn't realized she'd been holding.

He continued before she could speak. "I never heard either my mother or my father compliment the other."

"That might foster pride."

"They didn't use endearments or share a kiss in front of us kids." He kicked a clod of dirt out of the way.

Fannie let the conversation die. She had a great deal to think about.

When they reached home, Gideon left her to put the wagon away before going to work on the fence.

Fannie entered the kitchen where her aunts were busy cutting blocks of cured soap into bars. The lavender-scented batch perfumed the air. She took a deep breath, needing the relaxing properties attributed to lavender.

Happy to put her hands to work, Fannie gathered supplies and sat at the table to package the soap for sale at the flea market.

"Hello, dear." Aunt Lucy placed a tray of creamy bars in front of her. "Sarah saw the Schrocks have planted extra celery this year. Rows and rows of it."

Fannie fumbled the bar of soap she was wrapping in a crocheted washcloth. Arranging a smile on her face, she said, "That's *gut* news." Good news for Leah Schrock. The garden full of celery meant her wedding would take place this fall. Lucky Leah. She was marrying Eli Troyer.

"We're hoping there will be more than one wedding this fall," Aunt Susie added with a mischievous smile.

Fannie looked up. "Who else?" The question died on her lips.

The twinkle in Aunt Susie's eyes answered her question.

She looked down at the yarn she was tying to secure the washcloth around the bar of soap. "You have a wild imagination, Aunt Susie." She couldn't be angry with either of her dear aunts. They wanted her to be happy, but had they considered what they would do if she married? The possibility was so remote she felt silly raising the question. But she had to do something to get them to let go of their absurd notion that she would marry Gideon.

Taking another bar of soap, she carefully centered it on the washcloth. "Have you thought about who would help you with the Haus or the business if I was not here?"

Aunt Susie left the counter and came to sit beside Fannie. "That is none of your concern."

Fannie shrugged and measured another length of yarn. "I'm being practical." Why was everyone offering her advice on marriage today? First Prudy and now her aunts. *Must be something in the air.*

Aunt Susie took the yarn away from Fannie and held her hands. "If you have the opportunity to follow your heart, you are not to worry about us. We enjoy our business and the money it brings in. It keeps us busy and well cared for. Working with you is the most rewarding part. But if your dream for a husband and family of your own comes true, take hold of that dream with both hands."

Cheeks on fire, Fannie mumbled, "I don't think that's going to happen."

Aunt Susie squeezed her hands. "Why do you say that?"

"Ach." She tried to pull her hands from her aunt's grip, but the old woman was stronger than she looked. "Look at me!" The cry came from Fannie's heart. Tears welled and ran down her face.

"Oh, child." Aunt Susie clung harder. "I know you don't believe it, but you are beautiful. The right man will look beyond your scar and your limp. What he will see is a heart that shines like purest gold."

Fannie shook her head in disbelief. Her aunt was a dear, but she was looking at Fannie through eyes veiled with maternal love. "You raised me, Aunt Susie. You're the closest thing to a Mamm I have. That's why you're saying that."

Aunt Susie sighed. "I wish you could see yourself the way Lucy and I see you." Letting go of Fannie's hands, she rose and went back to the counter to continue slicing the block of soap.

Aunt Lucy slipped into the chair her sister had vacated. An air of sadness lay about her bent frame. "Don't dismiss an opportunity, Fannie." The seriousness in her aunt's voice held Fannie's attention. Avoiding eye contact, Aunt Lucy fiddled with one of the washcloths. "I did that and have lived with the regret."

Disbelief flowed through Fannie like a wave. "You?"

Aunt Lucy nodded. "I missed my chance with a nice young man well suited for me because I pinned all my hopes on another." She placed the washcloth back on the pile. "Love doesn't always look exactly like our expectations." She patted Fannie's hand. "Be open to what God has for you. That's all I'm saying." Standing, she returned to the kitchen counter.

Fannie packed the finished product into a storage tote, her thoughts in a whirl. She'd never known the reason why Aunt Lucy hadn't married. She'd assumed her aunt had never been interested in any of the local boys. To know her aunt had regrets about a deliberate choice she'd made was a travesty.

Snapping the lid on the tote, Fannie carried it into the room they used as an office. She paused to look out the window at the washhouse before turning away, shaking her head. Her aunts meant well. She just hoped they wouldn't be too disappointed when all their good intentions failed to bear fruit.

Gideon held a thick growth of wild grapevines aside for Fannie to duck through them. Goats trailed along in her footsteps. He hadn't expected an entourage when he'd invited Fannie to walk the fence line with him. He'd wanted to show her where he'd strengthened the fence and shored up posts. The curious goats had taken it upon themselves to chaperone the outing. They would stop to graze, then run to catch up, bells clanging.

"I think this section was the oldest part of the fence. The spot welds on the cross wire were weak, so I replaced it."

"Danke." She touched the shiny wire at the same time Petunia and Tulip pressed between her and the new fence.

"Do you think they're testing it?" He had the strange feeling the clever animals were listening to his every word and hatching a plan to show him that they were superior in their knowledge of fences.

Her soft chuckle sent warmth curling through his chest.

He was glad to hear her laugh. At supper she'd barely spoken, concentrating on her meal as though each bite were her last. No matter what he'd said to draw her out, she would only answer in monosyllables.

Her aunts, normally bubbling with plans and not-so-subtle attempts to bring him and Fannie together, were also subdued, causing him to review every minute of the day to find the reason behind the change of mood. As the only male at the table, having more to say than three women was disconcerting.

He found Fannie's thoughtfulness and depth of character appealing. On the walk to the Jameses', her attention had been solely on their conversation. She didn't have a cell phone to distract her. She wasn't concerned about her hair or clothing the way the English girls he'd dated had fussed over such things. She was a breath of fresh air, and he wanted to breathe her in like a drowning man.

He fell into step beside her. They walked through the tall grass and weeds to the corner where he'd replaced a post.

"Working on the fence has given me time to think about my return to Winsome."

Anxiety flashed in her eyes, and she turned her head away.

"I'm glad I came back, Fannie."

"You are?"

The doubt in her voice pained him. "I'm going to see the bishop tomorrow about receiving instruction so I can be baptized into the church."

She stopped and looked at him, eyes bright with hope. "Are you sure you're ready?"

"I want to rebuild what I destroyed when I left twelve years ago. Is that so hard to believe?"

"If you're baptized and change your mind, you'll be under the Bann," she said quietly.

He knew that. And if he was honest, a small part of him worried about that very thing. Though he was serious about returning, he wasn't hiding behind rose-colored glasses. "I'm sure there will be times I'll be frustrated. I'll wish for a car to drive or a cell phone. But if and when that happens, I'll deal with it." He petted a kid that ran up to him. "Every day I'm here strengthens my belief that I'm making the right decision." *I feel like I've found my home again.* He didn't say that, though. The sentiment sounded too hokey.

"What do you think will be the most difficult part about returning?"

Face the problem head-on. That was Fannie's straightforward way. Interesting that her question wasn't about what he would leave behind. Instead, she wanted to know what would be hard for him to come back to and, therefore, have to live with for the rest of his life. How wise of her.

He took his time thinking, wanting to get the answer to such an important question right. "Assuming I'm able to mend fences with my family, I believe the hardest part will be the reserved attitudes and manners of the people."

Uncertainty flickered across her features. "What do you mean?"

"Well," he paused to scratch behind Tulip's ears while she lipped the fabric of his pants leg. "This afternoon you were shocked by Prudy and Leland's affection for each other."

She looked down at the toes of her black shoes.

Determined to give an honest answer, he pressed on. "They were having a conversation, Fannie—expressing their appreciation of each other and their marriage. I'm not a reserved Amish man anymore. I'd be like Leland and not care who knew how much I loved my wife."

Her little squeak of embarrassment set off fireworks in his blood, surprising him in the process. So much for being circumspect and not shocking the daylights out of her. *But come on.* What was wrong with seeing a married couple share a quick kiss?

"Public displays are frowned upon." Her cheeks were a deep pink.

He wasn't sure if the color was due to embarrassment or a reflection of the setting sun turning the sky red-gold. Or perhaps a little of both. Either way, she looked beautiful with the wash of color.

"They were at home on their patio. Not downtown in front of city hall or something." He'd already made a hash of his explanation. Time to complete the job. "I want to be a good upstanding man in the community, Fannie, but at the same time, I've been away. I can't erase my past."

How he wished he could change some of the things that had happened. Seeing the bishop wouldn't turn the clock back. All he could hope for was the opportunity to call Winsome home once more.

6

The dew that fell overnight had vanished by the time Fannie got to work in the herb garden. The patch of horehound Aunt Lucy used as a medicinal had run wild, seeding wherever it took a notion. Fannie grasped a bunch of thick stems and yanked. The earth released the fibrous roots with a gentle spray of soil across her bare feet. The crushed leaves fragranced the air with a musky scent that tickled her nose. Tossing the stems into a bucket, she grabbed another wayward plant and pulled.

This chore had needed to be done for days now, but it had constantly moved to the bottom of her list. *Well, not today!* It was a perfect day for thinning and weeding. Uprooting plants and tossing them out matched her restless mood perfectly.

Yesterday had set her thoughts in disarray, flitting about like the butterflies in the garden. Thinking about Aunt Lucy's revelation was followed by brooding over Gideon's decision to visit the bishop to prepare for baptism into the church. From there, their discussion about Leland and Prudy popped into her head. Her mind skittered away from *that* embarrassing conversation only to land back on Aunt Lucy's confession.

Who would have guessed Aunt Lucy had lived all these years with a broken heart? Fannie's chest squeezed in sympathy for her elderly aunt and the hurt she'd carried inside. Beneath the good nature and humor, her heart ached with unfulfilled dreams.

The poor dear.

Aunt Susie approached carrying a pan of green beans to stem. "It's too beautiful a morning to stay indoors." She settled on the decorative stone bench at the edge of the herb garden.

Fannie tossed another handful of horehound into her bucket. Aunt Susie hadn't been shocked by Aunt Lucy's disclosure. "Tantchen, do others in the church know of Aunt Lucy's heartache?" The community was close-knit.

"Jah." Aunt Susie snapped back the stem end of the bean and then pulled the green string the length of it. With another quick snap, she took off the blossom end. "But that was a long time ago. Old memories fade."

Fannie paused the fierce uprooting of the willful horehound plants. Everyone would know which young man had pursued Aunt Lucy and been rebuffed, and which man she'd had her heart set on. "Are both men in the community?"

"Think of our ages." Aunt Susie paused snapping beans to look at Fannie. "There are few men our age left."

But there were enough. Aunt Susie's non-answer meant at least one of the two men was still alive.

"Aunt Lucy has had to spend a lifetime seeing them in the store, at frolics, on church Sunday." Tearing up a plant, Fannie chucked it in the bucket. "Their wives would have been her friends. She would have doted on their children and watched the little ones grow to have children of their own."

"Jah." Aunt Susie snapped both ends of another bean and dropped it into her stainless steel bowl. Her voice held a concerned note. "What's troubling you, Fannie?"

Fannie stared unseeing at her bare toes, dusted with rich loam. *Life continues to move forward.* Whether it was fast like the English world or at a slower pace like the Amish, nothing stayed exactly the same. People married. Babies were born. Elders died. For better or worse, lives continually changed.

"Gideon." Fannie jerked weeds from the circle of decorative rocks at the base of the birdbath. "He's so sure he can return to our simple life."

After caring for the goats and eating a hearty breakfast, he'd left to visit the bishop. Her aunts had packed him a raspberry turnover and a thermos of coffee before waving him off as though he were going across the country instead of a few miles down the road.

"And you're afraid he will not be able to give up his English ways?" Aunt Susie snapped another bean.

Fannie rose and walked over to the bench. With a sigh, she sat beside her aunt. "His time away has changed him." She watched Aunt Susie's fingers work swiftly over the bowl of green beans.

"Change comes to everyone, Fannie. That's part of life."

She snitched a bean and crunched on it. The burst of raw flavor was refreshing.

She had remained close to church and family. The changes in her life were traditional and expected. "Gideon has seen so much. He's done things I'll never have the opportunity to experience. He has ideas and opinions that are not Amish."

The thought of how easily Gideon spoke of Leland and Prudy's show of affection for each other made her blush. The longing for an enduring love feathered through her, followed by an unwelcome pinch of envy.

Aunt Susie patted Fannie's knee. "Don't let that scare you away from him. Have you ever thought maybe your views could use some stretching?"

Fannie gasped and stared at this woman who'd been her mother figure for so many years.

Aunt Susie brushed her hand through the air. "Ach. Take that shocked look off your face. As long as he lives within the bounds of the *Ordnung*, he'll do fine."

Fannie frowned. "I'm not sure if our talk has helped or hindered, Aunt Susie."

Her aunt waved a bean at her. "Well, let me know when you figure it out."

Fannie kissed her aunt's cheek and went back to weeding. Now she had her aunt's unconventional advice to add to the whirl of thoughts already in her head. When she finished this garden, she'd have to start on the vegetable patch to keep her sanity.

"Hi, *Tante* Fannie."

Startled, Fannie put out a hand to keep from falling headfirst into the horehound patch. "Micah! Mary! Don't sneak up on me like that."

Sarah's children stood next to Aunt Susie. The two of them were giggling.

Micah's grin showed a gap where he'd lost his two front teeth. Beneath the brim of his straw hat, his nose and cheeks were peppered with freckles. "Gotcha."

"Yes, you did, young man." Fannie frowned at Aunt Susie. "I'm assuming you put him up to that."

Eyes wide with innocence, Aunt Susie shook her head. "Not me. I'm just snapping beans."

Five-year-old Mary rubbed her hand across the spikes of lavender, then sniffed the oil on her skin. "Can we help?" Her hair was braided and pinned up into two loops in the back.

"I would appreciate that. Does your Mamm know you're here?" Time with Sarah's children was always a treat.

"Jah."

"Okay, then. Come help me weed around the birdbath." After showing them the difference between herbs and weeds, Fannie set them to work.

"Where's Gideon?" Micah pulled a weed and shook it, dislodging the moist soil clinging to the roots.

"He's visiting the bishop."

Micah inspected the weed he'd pulled before placing it in the bucket. "Daed says he's a good worker."

Fannie nodded in agreement. Samuel was a hard worker himself and would recognize that quality in someone else. "He's helped a great deal with the goats."

"Mamm wishes *Mammie* didn't hire him."

Fannie looked up at Aunt Susie's stunned face. Icy tendrils dispelled the warmth of the sun and crept across Fannie's back and shoulders. Sarah had made her dislike of Gideon no secret, but he'd done all the work asked of him and more. He had done nothing to cause concern. Was Sarah's own bitterness clouding her opinion of him?

And what of his *Bruder*? Fannie had seen with her own eyes how Abram had shunned Gideon. Were there others who didn't want him here?

She paused in her weeding. What about her? Was she finding it hard to accept the man Gideon had become because she was clinging to her childish fantasies? The prick of guilt caused tears to well in her eyes. Hastily she blinked them back. It appeared only Aunt Susie and Aunt Lucy had been willing to accept Gideon and give him a chance to prove himself.

Mary screeched and jumped back. Her face scrunched up in distaste. She pointed at the ground.

Knowing the girl's distaste for all things that crawled, Fannie exchanged a grin with Aunt Susie.

"What now, Mary?" Sounding like his father, Micah went to see what had upset his little sister. He squatted and studied the ground. "It's just a worm." He picked it up and let it dangle between his thumb and forefinger.

Mary howled and ran to find refuge behind Fannie.

"Ach." Fannie caught herself from tumbling sideways as Mary clung to her neck. Laughing, she put an arm around Mary and hugged the little girl close. "Little earthworms won't hurt you."

Micah cupped the offending invertebrate in his hand. "Daed says they plow the soil around the roots. It's their job."

"Your Daed is a wise man. God has given every one of His creations a job to do. That includes each of us."

Micah studied the worm before looking up at Fannie. "What's my job?"

"Right now, I think you're doing a fine job helping me."

Standing on one bare foot, Mary peeked around Fannie and stared at the worm in her brother's hand. "I don't like him. Put him back."

Micah dug a shallow hole, placed the worm inside and covered it over. Exhaling a long-suffering sigh, he asked, "What's Mary's job?"

Fannie bit back the chuckle tickling the back of her throat. "To help your Mamm and be your little sister."

Mary released her hold on Fannie, happy now that the worrisome worm was out of sight.

Micah poked at a weed before tugging it from the soil. "I do more than Mary. My jobs are more important."

Ah, pride. Squatting next to Micah, Fannie joined him in weeding around the decorative rocks at the base of the birdbath. "In God's eyes, what Mary does is as important as what you do. We don't decide what our job will be or its value. God alone defines our worth."

The words she spoke resonated in her spirit like a crashing cymbal. She touched the scar on her cheek with the tips of her dirt-coated fingers. Did she truly believe the words she said to Micah?

She looked up into Aunt Susie's twinkling eyes.

"Are you listening to yourself, Fannie?" Her aunt's smile was gentle.

From a distance came the *clip-clop* of horse's hooves. Beyond the waving green tips of the alfalfa field, a gray-top buggy pulled by a gleaming black horse moved at a brisk pace along the public road. Birds flitted in the maple tree. An orange barn cat stalked through the long grasses at the edge of the lawn.

Fannie took a deep breath. Her world looked the same, but inside she felt like she was perched on the brink of something extraordinary.

"Mammie?" Micah looked with longing toward the Grossdawdi Haus. "I'm hungry." His grandmother always had a treat waiting for him in the kitchen.

"Well then." Aunt Susie snapped her last green bean before handing him the bowl of bean ends. "Throw this into the compost heap, then come into the kitchen." She stood and took Mary's hand. "Come with me, Mary. I baked apple strudel yesterday. I saved two pieces hoping you and Micah would visit."

Fannie watched her aunt and the little ones go into the house before turning back to the weeding. With so many thoughts and feelings to sort out, she would be gardening the rest of the day.

Gideon took a sip of the coffee Susie had put in the thermos he carried. The hot liquid tasted good, so unlike Lucy's herbal tea. That stuff would peel paint.

He tried to remember the last time he'd walked any distance with a purpose in mind. He'd gotten so accustomed to hopping in his truck to go the shortest distance that this unhurried walk to the bishop's house gave him a new appreciation for the time to think. He had a lot of that to do.

He'd shocked Fannie talking about Leland and Prudy's relationship. Had his time in the English world really changed him so much, or had he never been reserved like most of the people in the settlement? How many were reserved in public, but outspoken at home? Now there was a question he'd have to ask Fannie—behind closed doors and all that.

On the heels of that conversation, he'd announced his intention to see the bishop. Her fear that he'd be baptized only to become disenchanted with the church again and be placed under the Bann was a very real worry. He couldn't make light of it. He knew what he was leaving. He fully expected there would be times he'd be exasperated by the unwritten rules that governed their everyday life.

After a great deal of thought, he had come to the conclusion that he would gladly suffer these momentary annoyances in order to be a part of his family again.

The wisdom to make this choice had come with growing up. More valuable than any of the stuff he was leaving behind were the people he had here. Including Fannie. In a few short days, the woman and her gentle ways had become important to him. A good Amish woman, she wouldn't consider him an outstanding prospect when picking a husband, but he was on the road to change that.

When he was welcomed back into the church, would she want anything to do with him? Probably not. A life with him would be a constant worry for her, wondering which rule he'd break next.

He wasn't a member of the church, and he was already experiencing the Bann with Abram. Though his brother may not call it that, it certainly looked like that was how he had felt at the hardware store the day before.

Across a field of potato plants, Gideon could see Bishop Esh's home. The old stone structure sat close to the road.

Gideon closed his thermos. This visit with the bishop would be his first step toward coming back into the church.

The path to the front door consisted of stepping-stones interspersed with creeping thyme. Each step released a strong herbal fragrance into the air.

The bishop's wife, Bonnie, opened the door and welcomed him inside.

Placing his hat on the peg next to the door and the thermos on the floor beneath it, he smoothed his hair. The scent of something tangy baking in the oven filled the house.

Bonnie motioned toward the sitting room. "Go right in. You'll stay after? I have a rhubarb-raisin pie in the oven."

"Thank you." The delicious sweet-and-sour pie had been one of his favorites when he was growing up.

Bishop Esh occupied the rocking chair, the seat of honor in the small sitting room. A Holy Bible lay open on the elderly man's knees. His gnarled hands rested on the thin pages. The balding top of his bowed head glistened in the natural light streaming through the window. The only sound in the room was the ticking of the ornately carved clock hanging on the wall.

Gideon took a seat in a straight-backed chair and waited silently, unsure if the bishop was praying or napping. He fought the urge to fidget. Stillness and patience were disciplines he'd lost in his years away. Now was as good a time as any to begin relearning them.

Bishop Esh looked up. Wisps of white hair and a thick beard framed his heavily lined face. "So you are here because you want to be welcomed back into our midst, Gideon Zook?" Intense pale-blue eyes seemed to probe deep into Gideon, searching for his intentions.

"I would like that. Yes." He was a grown man and shouldn't be so nervous, but the authority of the bishop was very real, and Gideon's return to the community depended on this man's goodwill.

"The reasons you left remain in place. The Ordnung governs our daily lives."

The Ordnung. The unwritten rules that held the community together by keeping the unwelcome influence of the English world at bay.

Gideon shifted in his chair. The unanswerable riddles surrounding the rules had driven him as a teen to question all he'd been taught. In the end, he'd made the difficult choice not to be baptized into the church. He'd left home rather than face the disappointment and censure of his family and friends.

He rubbed his palms on his thighs, determined to return with humility, honesty, and integrity. "It's true I don't understand why certain things are allowed and others are not."

Though not placed under the Bann, he'd known there would be those like his brother Abram who would exercise that discipline. Whether out of anger, self-righteousness, or the belief that practicing the Bann would strengthen the position of the church, Gideon didn't know.

The elderly bishop kept his silence for so long Gideon's heart sank into the pit of his stomach, sure he'd blown his chances of ever being accepted back.

Finally, the bishop spoke. "God chose not to isolate us. We are to be in the world, but not of the world. The English way of living advances at a fast pace. Too fast to properly manage, it appears."

Focusing on the wide floorboards gleaming in a patch of sunlight, Gideon considered the bishop's words.

Technology had outpaced the laws of the land. Drones were now the norm. Driverless cars would soon be on the road. Natural laws had been broken with the advent of cloning and artificial intelligence. Traditional ethical standards continued to be challenged at an alarming rate.

He looked up at Bishop Esh. "What you say is true."

The elder stroked his beard. "To survive, we adapt. We make changes, but those changes take place over time, after a great deal of thought." He speared Gideon with a discerning look. "Often we move too slowly for young men filled with the energy and eagerness of youth."

Ouch. Taking the reprimand in stride, Gideon allowed himself a smile of acknowledgment. "But now that I'm an adult, I see the world differently, right?"

"Only you can answer that question." Bishop Esh closed the Bible and held it with both hands. "Electricity and cars are not sinful in and of themselves. They are tools. But allowing them into our homes, our barns, and our businesses would cause erosion to our way of life. Think of the soil. If good practices are not followed and erosion occurs, soon the soil is swept away and there is nothing left to till. No soil to plant in means no crop to harvest. If we allow the erosion of our culture, our traditions, and our values, we become like the world."

"I've been gone so many years. Where do I begin?" Gideon had asked himself that question many times, and it felt good to ask it out loud to someone who could answer him.

The bishop rocked in his chair. "Where you first began your life among the people. Mend your ties to your family."

Gideon wanted the answer to be less difficult than facing the old wounds of his rebellion. His Mamm and Daed had devoted their life to God and the church. They had wanted the best for him and his brothers. Leaving the way he had made him guilty of disobedience to his parents. The time had come to humble himself and ask for their forgiveness. In fact, it was much overdue.

The pit of his stomach curled with sick dread. In addition to speaking face-to-face with his family, he had to speak of his good friend, Jacob King. Their shared Amish background had been the bond that kept them together as they worked jobs in the city. It was long past time he visited Jacob's family. Gideon's heart constricted. They needed to know the details of how their son had died.

7

Fannie's green skirt whipped about her legs. She hurried along the lane to Sarah's house with her wooden wagon rumbling at her heels. Ruby-red jars of pickled beets rocked back and forth, cushioned by pages torn from old copies of *The Budget*.

Sarah and Samuel were hosting church the coming Sunday, just two days away. The flurry of cleaning necessary for the occasion had exhausted everyone in the family. Today Sarah planned on washing windows. Which meant Fannie would be washing windows.

The strings on her Kapp fluttered about her shoulders. The morning's soft air held the promise of a warm afternoon under a clear sky. She was thankful rain was not in the forecast. All the cleaning that had been done this week could easily come undone with wet weather and mud.

Yesterday the aunts had turned their efforts away from the cleaning and onto the task of baking. This morning the Grossdawdi Haus was filled with the delicious scent of cinnamon and apples. They were baking schnitz pies to serve at the fellowship meal following the service.

Whispering a prayer of thanksgiving for the close friends that would bring additional food, Fannie picked up her pace. Sarah would be frantic that the day's tasks had not yet begun.

Gideon had left the Grossdawdi Haus right after the barn chores to help Samuel. The men had spent the week sprucing up the yard and outbuildings. The chicken coop had received a new coat of paint. The barn and farming equipment had been set in order.

Today they were removing the last of the bulky furniture on the first floor of the house and storing it in the shed. The church bench wagon would arrive tomorrow. Samuel and Gideon, with the help of two other men, would be setting the benches in place for the service.

Fannie waved away a persistent fly. When the men finished, she'd no doubt have another quick sweep and mop to do. With so many work boots tramping through the house, someone was bound to leave traces of the yard behind.

"Aunt Fannie!" Micah and Mary ran to greet her, free-range chickens scattering before them in a whirl of feathers and dust. With childish enthusiasm, they jumped and ran circles around Fannie and her wagon. Both children had contributed to the cleaning effort by doing work appropriate for their ages.

Jabbering about the friends they would see on Sunday, the children seemed to have forgotten that the service beforehand felt as though it stretched unending when one had to sit quietly for three long hours.

Fannie brought the wagon to a halt at the kitchen door. "Help me bring in the jars." Propping open the screen door, she handed each child a jar of beets before following them indoors with her arms full. They set the jars on the kitchen table.

"Fannie, is that you?" Sarah sounded anxious.

"Finish bringing in the jars, please," Fannie instructed her helpers, "then close the door so the chickens don't come in uninvited." Fannie walked across the black-and-white checked linoleum floor and entered the sitting room. In the corner, Sarah stood on a step stool dusting the crown of the grandfather clock.

"Get down from there!" Fannie scolded, trotting to her cousin's side. "You shouldn't be climbing like this." She reached up to help Sarah down. "If you fall, we'll both be in trouble with Aunt Susie, not to mention that husband of yours."

Ignoring her, Sarah ran a soft cloth over the dark walnut wood.

"We aren't moving the clock to the barn. I'm so afraid something will happen to it."

"Of course it's not going to the barn. The clock has never been moved for church." The clock had occupied that same corner from Fannie's earliest memory. She'd come to visit with her own Mamm and Daed, and been enthralled by the huge timepiece with its swinging pendulum and loud ticking. "Now please climb down."

The thought of moving the clock was irrational, but over the last few days Sarah had worked herself into a senseless frenzy.

With one last swipe of her cloth, Sarah placed a hand on Fannie's shoulder to step off the stool.

Tightening her hold, Fannie felt the rolling movement of Sarah's baby beneath her hand. "Oh." She laughed, not moving her hand though Sarah had safely placed both feet on the floor.

Moisture beaded on Sarah's brow. "Another six weeks, Fannie. I'm not sure I'll make it. This one moves a lot more than any of the others at this stage."

Taking the cloth from her cousin, Fannie urged her into the kitchen. "Of course you will." She pulled out a chair from the table. "Sit. I'll get you something to drink."

Sarah sank into the chair and sighed. "This is my first summer baby. Such a busy time with so much to do, and then church Sunday on top of everything else."

Fannie set a glass of tart homemade lemonade on the table in front of Sarah. "That's why we're here to help you. And as the weeks go on, we'll help you more."

"Danke." Sarah took a sip from the glass. "I guess it's silly to worry."

It was, but Fannie knew better than to agree out loud. She would do the work at hand today and let tomorrow take care of itself. "I'll start the windows."

Being careful not to fall off the step stool, Fannie passed the window shade to Sarah. Running her dust rag across the lintel, she set to work cleaning the panes of glass until they sparkled in the sunlight.

"I think I see a smudge in that corner." Sarah pointed to the upper right.

Fannie dutifully spritzed more cleaning fluid on the glass and rubbed harder. Over the last two hours, Sarah had grown increasingly argumentative. Taking the shade from Sarah, Fannie slipped the end pins into the bracket nailed to the window frame.

Sarah tested the spring in the shade by lowering and raising it twice. "You know how important this day is for me." Her words echoed in the empty room.

"It's important to all of us." Fannie was heartily tired of the subject. They had batted this litany back and forth every day since the cleaning began. But this afternoon—after they'd shared a light lunch outdoors with Samuel, Gideon, and the children—Sarah had become increasingly obsessed with the subject. Something was bothering her. Something more than her aching back.

Dipping her cleaning cloth in a pan of warm water, Sarah wrung it out like her life depended on it. "This is more than a church service. It's also a home inspection."

Fannie repeated what she'd said the last ten times Sarah had voiced that fact. "You have nothing to worry about." Spraying the window, she climbed onto the stool to reach the very top. "There is nothing in your home prohibited by the Ordnung. And Samuel has only the approved equipment in the barn and shed." Fannie gave the window a final swipe. Working up her courage, she finally asked, "What's truly bothering you, Sarah?"

Sarah tossed her cloth in the bucket. Sudsy water splashed over the edges and onto the floor. "If you must know, Gideon's presence here is upsetting me."

Fannie carefully climbed off the stool. Her knees wobbled like she'd run a mile. "He grew up in the church. He won't embarrass us, if that's your worry."

"What will people think?" Having finally admitted what was preying on her mind, Sarah kept talking as if Fannie hadn't said a word. "Abram will be here. I don't need a family fight on the front lawn."

Fannie's giggle came out as a nervous titter. "*When* have you seen such a thing? We do not fight. You know that. We ignore. We avoid. We endure. But we do not fight. There will not be a brawl on the front lawn." *At least, I hope not.*

Sarah continued expressing her dreadful thoughts. "Can you imagine what would be said? The service would be remembered and whispered about *forever.*"

Having a special memory of a church service would certainly make life interesting. Fannie still smiled over such an incident from her childhood. One of the elderly ministers seated at the end of minister's row had fallen asleep during the second sermon. He'd toppled off the backless bench and onto the floor. Those sitting close by had helped him back onto the bench. The minister preaching that day never paused in his delivery of the sermon. The service continued on as though nothing out of the ordinary had happened.

Of course, a family conflict would not be something to smile about, so Fannie wisely kept her thoughts to herself. "Do you want me to speak to Gideon?"

Sarah's eyes homed in on Fannie and narrowed. "You? He's Mamm's hired man. Shouldn't she talk to him?" Suspicion snaked through Sarah's voice. "When do you see him to talk to? Isn't he in the barn taking care of the goats?"

"He does all the heavy labor and helps with the milking." Fannie covered her scar.

"I warned you about him." Sarah huffed.

Fight or flight. Fannie had never learned to fight. Flight was difficult without wings, but as long as she could move . . . She picked up her stool and bucket, and walked to the next window. "I have to show him all there is to do."

Sarah followed on Fannie's heels. "Are Mamm and Aunt Lucy playing at making a match for you?"

Fannie scrambled up on the stool wishing she had a saucy comeback that would quiet Sarah's tongue.

"You're blushing." Sarah exhaled a long dramatic sigh. "Oh, Fannie. He's been English for a long time. A plain woman will not hold his interest." To emphasize her words, Sarah tugged on the hem of Fannie's chore apron. "He'll grow tired of doing things the old way and will soon be gone again."

Fannie rubbed the glass so hard it squeaked beneath her cloth. Sarah was just being Sarah, but bossier and fussier than usual because of her condition and her stress.

Unsure whom she needed to convince, Fannie looked down at her cousin. "He went to visit Bishop Esh."

The statement hung heavy in the air between them. To seek the bishop's counsel was a huge decision.

Sarah stared up at her for a long moment before speaking. "When?"

Fannie climbed down. "They talked at the start of the week."

"About being baptized?" Her work forgotten, Sarah followed Fannie into the first-floor bedroom, now empty of all furniture.

"What did the bishop say?"

Fannie set her bucket down on the floor. "He didn't tell me, and I didn't ask." She frowned at Sarah. "You know that whatever is said to the bishop is private."

Sarah shrugged one shoulder and looked sidelong at Fannie. "I thought since you were working so closely, he would have told you."

Fannie ignored Sarah's remark. Even if she had known what they'd talked about, she wouldn't break the confidence. But Gideon hadn't shared any part of his meeting with the bishop.

Since that day, Gideon had been more thoughtful going about his work. In conversation, he weighed his words and listened closely as if trying to read the thoughts behind her words. Was he comparing her to an English woman he'd met?

She had made it clear to him she didn't trust him or his motives for returning. Why should he trust her with his innermost thoughts?

Saturday morning passed swiftly for Gideon. He helped Samuel at the main house by mowing the lawn and trimming around trees and fence posts. He took a seat in a lawn chair in the cool shade of the maple tree. His damp shirt clung to his back.

Little Mary Yoder served him and her father thick ham sandwiches on dinner plates.

Careful not to let the lopsided slice of ham fall out of the soft bread that had torn when she cut it, Gideon took a bite. What the sandwich lacked in presentation, it more than made up for in flavor.

With her big blue eyes watching, he made a production of chewing the home-cured ham and home-baked bread. After swallowing he said,

"You make a delicious ham sandwich, Mary. Thank you."

Happy with his verdict, she ran into the house where her Mamm and Fannie continued the work of preparing for church tomorrow.

Over the years he'd spent running from his Amish roots, Gideon had missed the food second only to missing his family. Since his return, he'd eaten his fill. Susie Lapp and Lucy Miller were excellent cooks and more than happy to stuff him like a Thanksgiving turkey—so much so, in fact, that his trousers were getting tight around the waist.

"The church wagon will be here soon." Samuel sat beside him, putting his hat on the grass beneath his chair.

"You'll have to show me where to put the benches." Helping Samuel prepare for the occasion had brought back long-buried memories of when his own Mamm and Daed had hosted church Sunday. They were good memories, and he hoped in the future to make many more.

Samuel took a long drink from his glass of lemonade. "Your brother will be here tomorrow."

"Yes." Gideon looked forward to seeing his brother. He hoped there would be an opportunity to talk.

"I've told Sarah I don't believe there will be a problem, but she's concerned."

From the end of the lane came the rumble of a large wagon pulled by a team of draft horses.

Gideon stood and slapped his hat back on his head. "I'd like to talk to Abram tomorrow, but if that happens, it will be because he came to me. Tell Sarah there will be no trouble."

The church wagon pulled into the yard followed by an open-top carriage.

Gideon recognized an old friend, Brian Fisher, driving the team that pulled the big, boxy wagon.

Brian jumped down and greeted Samuel. He turned to Gideon.

"Wilkum." Brian extended his hand.

Gideon took it, grateful a cold shoulder hadn't been turned his way.

"You remember my Daed." Brian indicated the older man stepping out of the carriage that had followed the church wagon.

Gideon greeted Brian's father. The feeling that he'd been left behind swept over him. He ran a hand over his jaw, bare as that of a fresh-faced youth. The long beard on his friend's face signified several years of marriage. While he'd been away working and experiencing what the world had to offer, Brian had built a life in the community.

Brian walked around the back of the wagon and unlatched the door. "There's word you're coming back to us."

Gideon helped him slide the first bench out of the wagon. "That's the goal."

"If you want help with anything, let me know." Brian reached into the wagon for the next bench and handed it to his father.

With the future looming like a big question mark, Gideon was grateful for the offer. "Thank you."

Following the other men, he helped set up the benches in the traditional arrangement. As they worked, he caught glimpses of Fannie in the kitchen and his heart swelled.

After many trips back and forth between the wagon and the house, the benches were in place. The only items left to bring indoors were cartons filled with hymnals.

After saying goodbye to Brian and his father, Gideon carried one of the cartons indoors and set it on a bench. Curious to see another piece of his past, he pulled back the flaps and took out an *Ausbund*. He ran his hands along the worn edges of the black cover and thumbed through the pages. He hadn't read German in years. The words looked familiar and at the same time foreign. Someone entered the room, and he looked up.

Fannie stood inside the kitchen door with a broom in her hand. She smiled and came in to sit on the bench beside him. "You're sitting on the women's side." The gold flecks in her brown eyes twinkled.

He returned her smile. "I didn't think that mattered today. I'll follow tradition tomorrow." Fanning the pages of the Ausbund, he inhaled the musty scent.

Fannie bumped against him with her shoulder. "A penny for them."

Recognizing his own words being tossed back at him, he shrugged. "Did you know the first printing of this book was back in the 1500s?"

The sun streaming through the window got caught in her hair not covered by her Kapp. The molasses-colored strands glinted red and gold. She looked at him with big brown eyes but didn't comment. She didn't run away either, which he took as an invitation to keep talking.

"Years of persecution led to our traditions." He had no idea where he was going with this train of thought, but he kept on doggedly. "We sing the same songs in the same slow way, though we no longer have to fear being discovered." He closed the book. "Why? Why do we continue to live the old way?"

Eyes downcast, she remained silent.

"I guess I'm still trying to work out the riddles that plagued me when I left Winsome."

The woman sitting at his side had blindly followed the traditions all her life, never questioning the way things were done or why they were done at all. He, on the other hand, had spent most of his life asking questions. He was still asking them.

When Fannie finally spoke, her voice was a mere whisper. "The traditions keep us connected to our roots." She glanced at him and then folded both hands in her lap. "Hundreds of years have passed, and we continue to carry the burden of all those lives that were lost in the persecution. It's right that we remember and honor their struggle to find religious freedom."

She rubbed the palms of her hands over the rose-colored fabric covering her knees. The backs of her hands were red and chapped from the cleaning she'd done this week. "We're still here, and we are still worshiping God because we continue to follow the Ordnung. We keep the traditions. We must never forget where we came from."

Gideon stared at the hymnal he held in both hands. "Otherwise we'd be absorbed by the world. No longer set apart."

The children's laughter came through the open window. Micah and Mary were playing a game of tag in the yard. Sarah worked in the kitchen while talking to baby Malachi. Tomorrow this room would be filled with people.

He turned to Fannie. "Thank you."

"Why are you thanking me?" she asked, her eyes wide.

"You didn't run away. You didn't dismiss my rambling or tell me I shouldn't question." He set the hymnal on the bench. "You don't make me feel like I don't measure up because I have questions."

Fannie clasped her hands together. The light in her eyes had grown dim as they talked. "I don't trust that your return to the settlement is the best choice, or indeed, possible, Gideon." Her knuckles whitened. "But, if you choose to come back, you must do so with your eyes open."

"You're right." He wondered what it cost her to be so blunt. "I appreciate your willingness to listen without judging me and telling me I'm forever lost for even thinking about these things."

"God never gives up on us. How can I do any less for you?" Her eyes grew wide as if she'd surprised herself.

In truth, she'd astonished him. "So which is it, Fannie? First you tell me you don't think coming back is a good idea. You think I'll fail and leave under the Bann. Yet, you aren't giving up on me. So maybe you do think I could be successful?"

She just stared back at him, brown eyes wide.

The confusion in her face matched the turmoil he felt. He'd ripped his heart out of his chest and attached it to his sleeve. If she didn't think less of him before, she would now. "Guess there are no easy answers."

Fannie nodded and dropped her gaze.

Looking beyond Fannie, he saw Sarah glaring at him from the kitchen doorway. He stood. "I'm keeping you from your work."

This conversation hadn't been one of his finer moments. Stepping from between the benches, he headed for the door.

Gideon was sweeping the last of the dirt from the ramp leading into the barn when a shadow fell across his push broom.

Sarah stood on the end of the ramp, a dish towel in her hand. "You need to leave."

He continued working. "I'll be done in a few minutes. Supper at your Mamm's isn't for another half hour. I have time."

"No. I mean you have to leave the farm." She stepped closer. "I don't want you here."

"Your mother hired me. If she decides to let me go, I will go." He leaned on the broom. "But not until then."

Huffing, Sarah twisted the dish towel in her hands. "My mother doesn't know you like I do. I was a witness to your running-around years."

A good Amish man would avoid this confrontation. Gideon knew he should walk away, but he couldn't. He wasn't that noble. "As I was a witness to yours."

The color drained from her face.

Nailed it. Rebellion against church rules had been his crowd's singular goal.

"Regrets are a given," he said.

"No one talks about those days."

"The code of silence practiced by generations. Got it. What happened never happened." Gideon gave the broom a shove. "Except it did."

Recovering her composure, Sarah crossed her arms over her large middle. "I'm surprised you came back."

Finished sweeping, Gideon banged the brush of the broom against the cement ramp to dislodge remnants of dirt and dust. He looked at her. "I'm surprised you're still here after what happened during your running-around years."

8

Aunt Susie and Aunt Lucy chattered in Pennsylvania Dutch while passing a platter of apple pancakes followed by warm maple syrup, freshly churned goat butter, and chunky applesauce.

Fannie helped herself to pancakes. Sunday morning was never the best day to eat a heavy breakfast. She would be hard-pressed to stay awake during the service, especially after having a sleepless night. Her conversation with Gideon while at Sarah's house yesterday had circled round and round in her mind like the hands of a clock.

His questions were unsettling, and not only because he'd actually voiced them. She'd responded with the answers she had heard all her life, but they sounded too simple. And now, here she sat, wondering why she had never questioned the church traditions or the Ordnung. Her insides quivered with anxiety. If the bishop ever found out what she was thinking—*mercy!*

Gideon bore dark circles under his eyes and had appeared preoccupied during the milking this morning. Fannie couldn't be sure which had caused his lack of sleep. Did yesterday's conversation continue to trouble him, or was it facing the crowd at church today?

Spooning warm applesauce over her pancakes, she sneaked a glance at him and got caught in the light green of his eyes. Her heart stumbled in her chest.

He held her gaze for a few breathless moments before looking down at his plate. "Yesterday I told Samuel I'd be over as soon as we finished breakfast."

"*Gut.*" Aunt Susie finished pouring cream in her coffee and plunked the pitcher on the table. "Fannie will walk with you. Lucy will help me with dishes."

"Jah." Aunt Lucy chimed in.

Fannie's fork stopped halfway to her mouth. "But Gideon may not want to walk with me." The words came out in a stammering rush.

Gideon raised an eyebrow. "Why wouldn't I want to walk with you?"

Oh dear. "I-I mean, maybe you don't have time to wait for me. I have to change into my Sunday dress."

Aunt Lucy dabbed maple syrup from her lips and exchanged a furtive smile with her sister. "Fannie, of all the people I know, you take the least amount of time to get ready to go places."

Not knowing if her aunt meant that as a compliment, Fannie set her fork down, her appetite gone.

Her aunts meant well, but she'd had enough of being told what to do. Maybe because she'd spent the better part of the last week in Sarah's presence. Whatever the reason, she didn't want to be dumped on Gideon. She put her hand to her cheek. "I would prefer to have Gideon make the choice."

Aunt Susie's fork clattered on her plate, and Aunt Lucy's eyebrows jumped practically to her hairline.

Gideon stopped slathering butter on his stack of pancakes and stared at her.

With the little courage she had left, she lifted her chin and held his gaze. His silence unnerved her. She was preparing to flee the room when he spoke.

"I would be happy if you walked with me, Fannie." His smile flickered on and off so fast she almost missed it. "But I want you to make the choice. Not your aunts. Not me. You choose."

Fannie blinked. Uncertainty twisted in the pit of her stomach. What did she want to do? For one unkind moment, she wanted to refuse just to spite her aunts and their blatant meddling. But, truthfully, a tired body and weary mind were leading the way with that train of thought. She'd regret anything she said the minute the words left her mouth.

Unmoving, Gideon watched and waited for her reply.

Fannie's heart raced. Walking to church with Gideon would be the fulfillment of one of her girlish dreams. All she needed was the courage to speak up. She took a calming breath. "I can be ready to go by the time you finish eating breakfast."

Without looking at him or her aunts, she rose and hurried from the room.

Though she'd barely eaten a mouthful of her breakfast, hunger wasn't what caused the curling sensation in Fannie's tummy. The opportunity to walk to church at Gideon's side was having the strangest effect on her senses.

In her newest plum-colored dress, Fannie raced passed the kitchen doorway without a word to her aunts. Gideon was waiting for her on the porch. He was dressed in black trousers, white shirt, and a vest.

She followed him down the steps to the gravel lane, still embarrassed by her outburst at the breakfast table.

Away from the house, he spoke. "You amazed me this morning, Fannie, sticking up for yourself." His voice held gentle approval.

Her heart did a funny little cartwheel. Of all the things she'd expected Gideon to say, that was not one of them. She couldn't look at him. "Oh." *Brilliant, Fannie.* "Danke." She whispered the word afraid to break the bubble of happiness surrounding her.

Gideon kicked a pebble in the lane. "I haven't been very good company this morning."

Fannie shrugged. "That's okay. You look tired."

"So do you." He smiled. "Guess we both lost sleep last night."

"Jah."

"So which one of us goes first, you or me?"

"What?" She was still stuck on the idea she'd amazed him.

"I'll go first." He looked across the hayfield gathering his thoughts. "Yesterday, setting up the benches and holding a copy of the Ausbund for the first time in twelve years, well, the reality of what I intend to do hit me hard."

Fannie rubbed her fingers across her scar. She wanted him to stop talking. She didn't want to hear any more.

Unaware of the effect his words were having on her, Gideon continued. "I knew coming home would be difficult. I didn't realize to what extent."

Her heart sank. Was he going to leave? She wanted to curl up and protect the little girl inside who was going to lose another person she loved—or rather, losing someone a second time. "Do you regret that you came home?"

"No." His direct gaze held a challenge. "But I know I will never be the perfect Amish man."

There wasn't an Amish man in all of Winsome that she'd consider perfect, except for maybe Gideon. The thought sent a shock wave of astonishment through her.

He gave a sheepish chuckle. "I'm nervous about seeing everyone today."

"Your parents are still visiting Joshua and his family, but Abram will be at church."

"Yeah." Gideon took off his felt hat and resettled it on his head. "I promised Samuel there would be no brawling on his lawn."

Fannie clapped her hand over her mouth in shock and glanced sidelong at him. The man was spinning her emotions in all directions.

"Your turn. What kept you up last night?"

She dropped her hand to her side. "All your questions." She stopped walking, needing a moment to figure out how to put her thoughts into words that felt like blasphemy. "Do you think I'm foolish to follow the Ordnung without questioning any of the rules?"

Rooted in place, Fannie held her breath waiting for the earth to shift beneath her feet or the sky to rain down thunderbolts. When neither cataclysmic event happened, she exhaled and dared to look at Gideon.

He stepped closer. The warmth in his eyes set her pulse racing. "I think, Fannie Lapp, that your faith and the boundaries you choose to live within give you strength of character that I envy, sinful as that may be."

The tip of his finger touched her hair. He traced the edge of her prayer covering. "You are not a fool for living the life you were born to live."

His smile warmed Fannie to her toes. Her insides melted like butter in a hot skillet. *Don't ever leave us again. Don't leave me again.* She didn't dare utter those words. Instead she said, "What about you? Weren't you born to live this life too?"

Gideon stood at Samuel's side waiting for the first families to arrive for church. From this vantage point on the ramp into the barn, they could look across the distance and see buggies moving along the roads intersected by fields. Closer to the farm, couples and families walked the lanes making their way to church in the morning sunshine.

"Sarah has been up since before dawn, fussing over the food and children." Samuel swatted at a fly buzzing loudly in the Sunday morning stillness.

Gideon absorbed the warmth of the sunshine, recalling his own mother's agonizing over hosting church Sunday. "Fannie will calm her down." He didn't question how he knew this. He only knew what he said was the truth. All would go well for Sarah because Fannie was there.

Walking to church side by side had felt like the most natural thing in the world. He realized he no longer noticed the scar on her cheek or the limp in her walk—they were simply part of her. The way the morning sun found glints of red in her brown hair and her quick smile now held his attention.

She'd shocked him this morning with her question. Had his struggle set her on the path of dissatisfaction with her life? And what if he decided to come back only to be faced with her decision to leave the community? His heart dropped with a sickening thud. The last thing he had meant for her to do was question her beliefs. Could this be another sin that would require atonement?

The first buggy turned off the road. The standardbred bay trotted at a good clip into the yard and stopped at the house to let the women and children off before continuing on.

Serving as Samuel's hostler for the day gave Gideon the opportunity to greet the men of the church district before the service started. Many were familiar faces. Though seeming glad to see him, they were reserved in their welcome.

As more families arrived for church, the ache in Gideon's chest bloomed. The boys he'd grown up with were now married men with children. Men not much older than he had streaks of silver in their beards that had not been there twelve years ago. Elders stooped with age gathered in a small knot, their wide hat brims hiding their faces.

Talk concerning crops, weather, and livestock set Gideon awash in nostalgia. The art of visiting and caring for one another was evident in this gathering of men.

A lump formed in Gideon's throat. Though the men were cordial and didn't purposely exclude him, he shared no commonality with them. He'd removed himself from the community, and his bonds to this brotherhood had been severed.

He was leading Bishop Esh's horse when he heard Abram's distinctive laugh. Clamping down on the maelstrom of emotion that would surely be communicated to the horse, Gideon took a deep breath and kept walking. He'd promised Samuel there would be no drama, but the longing to say hello and have a conversation with his brother was overwhelming.

Not long after Abram's arrival, the ministers signaled the time had come to go into the house. Following tradition, the ministers and elders entered first followed by the married men. Not part of that group, Gideon fell into line when an unbaptized youth deferred to age and motioned for Gideon to enter before him and the other boys.

Unsettled, Gideon walked into the house. He was dressed plain and looked like the other men, but he wasn't married. He wasn't baptized. He wasn't part of the community. He didn't belong, just as he hadn't fully belonged in the English world.

The women were already seated on their side of the room. Fannie sat among them, quiet and ready to worship.

He caught her eye and a wisp of a smile passed over her lips before she looked away. Eye contact was discouraged during the service. This was meant to be a time of reflection and reverence. God the Almighty was the focus and would be for the next three hours.

Today, Samuel had been chosen to lead the songs. Sitting with the men, he sang the first few notes of each line, with the congregation following his lead and joining in.

Gideon struggled through the first song, the slow tempo at odds with the tension humming through him. The Ausbund open in his hand, his tongue stumbled over the German. With no musical score to follow, he gave himself up to the cadence of the words and accompanied the voices filling the room.

The second song of the service, *Das Loblied*, had always been his favorite. During this hymn of praise the tension he carried in his shoulders and chest seeped away.

The music ended, and the noise and disruption of kneeling for prayer rose like a holy tumult followed by silence. Gideon couldn't remember the last time he'd kneeled in God's presence. He'd said prayers on the fly. He'd sat at his kitchen table and prayed. He'd prayed while driving his truck. But something about actually kneeling focused a man's heart on the Divine.

He'd forgotten that. Or maybe he'd never fully appreciated kneeling for prayer as a kid. But here in this room, the hard floor beneath his knees, a reverence for the Lord Almighty welled up inside him and spilled over in silent tears.

The scrape of the minister's shoe on the floor signaled everyone to rise from their knees and sit on the benches again.

Swiping under his eyes, Gideon glanced at Fannie. Their gazes connected. Seeing his watery eyes, hers grew round.

Smiling sheepishly, Gideon looked down at his hands. He didn't want to get her in trouble. For all his worry yesterday, the conviction that he had made the right choice in coming home settled firmly in his heart.

Time passed swiftly for Gideon, and soon the service came to a close. Folks were clearing out of the house so the benches could be converted to tables and seating for the fellowship meal. Before he could get out of the room, Lucy appeared at his elbow.

"Gideon, will you help carry the cooler of lemonade to the table outdoors?"

With his throat dry from sitting for hours in close quarters with the other worshipers, Gideon welcomed the detour into the kitchen. He would beg a sample of the lemonade before carrying it outside where the older boys gathered while their elders were served their meal.

Sarah stood at the kitchen counter handing off bowls and platters of food to a stream of chatty women.

Another man stood in the kitchen talking to Susie.

Recognizing the set of his brother's shoulders, Gideon stopped short.

"Keep moving, young man." Lucy gave him a firm shove from behind, setting his feet in motion once more.

He'd been set up.

Gideon grasped the cooler handle closest to him, tension once again humming through him.

Unaware of Gideon's presence, Abram laughed at something Susie said before turning to reach for the cooler. He jerked to a stop as his eyes flashed with recognition. The smile on his lips flattened in a straight line.

"Hello, Abram."

Anger simmered in his brother's eyes.

Acknowledging Gideon with a curt nod, he grasped the cooler's other handle. Together they lifted it from the counter. Gideon dropped back letting Abram lead the way outdoors.

Dressed in raspberry-colored dresses with matching capes and aprons, Lucy and Susie followed after them like two tiny hummingbirds. Darting past the two men, they made room on the table for the cooler. Setting a stack of paper cups next to it, Susie clasped her hands together and stood her ground in front of the two men.

"Abram, it's good to see Gideon. Jah?"

Backed up against the table by two elderly women, Abram stood straight and silent. All around them, conversation had halted and all movement in the crowd was suspended.

Unable to resist the opportunity, Gideon hoped a soft voice would turn away his brother's wrath. "It's good to see you, Abram. I hope we have a time to speak in private soon."

Without a word, Abram sidestepped Gideon and the aunts, and walked away to join a small group of men waiting for their turn to sit at the tables and eat.

Appearing crestfallen, the two elderly sisters held hands as if gathering strength from each other.

The sadness on their lined faces tugged at Gideon's heart.

"Don't be disappointed, please." Setting aside his own heartache, he tried to ease their distress. "I'll be reconciled with my family in God's own time."

"Jah. In God's time." Lucy patted her sister's hand and together they set off to join Sarah and the others already serving the ordained men and elders.

"Did you enjoy your first preaching Sunday back with us?" Fannie's skirt swished with each step. The midafternoon had a warm, dusty smell to it.

Walking at her side, Gideon considered her question. "I wouldn't say *enjoyed* is the right word."

"What then?" She walked so close, her shoulder bumped his arm.

"I felt out of place with the other men. In church, things came back slowly at first, but then we sang *Das Loblied* and kneeled to pray." He shrugged.

Her dark-brown eyes captured his and held. "You cried."

He marveled that he didn't feel a smidge of embarrassment that she'd caught him teary-eyed. "Jah." Startled that the old familiar word had come out of his mouth, he blinked hard. "Yes. God's presence felt very real today."

A smile warmed her expression. "That's *gut*." Fannie picked a dandelion and twirled the stem between her fingers. "Everyone is looking forward to the barn frolic. It's unfortunate our good time comes because someone's barn burned down."

Relieved she'd changed the subject, he turned his thoughts to the barn raising that was to take place in a little over two weeks. The bishop had announced it at the end of service. It had been the talk of the fellowship dinner. Abram would be there. He hoped Jacob's family would be there too. Though they lived in the next church district, they were close enough to consider lending a hand while enjoying time with family and friends.

Gideon rubbed his hand across the back of his neck. The time had come to tell Fannie about Jacob. "While I worked in the city, I had a close friend. Jacob King."

"That's a *gut* Amish name." Curiosity shaded her voice.

"He'd left the plain life, like I did. We met on a construction site. We had a common background, so we became close friends."

A frown furrowed her brow. "A little taste of home, I imagine?"

"Yes." Gideon forced himself to continue. "If you want to build something new in the city, you must tear down what is already on the land. Often we took down historic buildings filled with beautiful woodwork made by craftsman before the use of power tools."

"They must have been lovely."

Gideon nodded in agreement. "Salvage companies would come in and take the architectural gems."

"Like what?"

"Marble fireplaces. Stained glass windows. There's a market for period pieces." Gideon had seen beautiful craftsmanship in those old buildings. "Once those items were stripped from the building, I ran the excavator and tore it down. The money was good. I consoled myself with that."

She snorted indelicately. "The love of money, Gideon?"

He shrugged. "Living in the city is expensive. But eventually, that excuse—along with a host of others—no longer eased my conscience."

"So you stopped?"

He wished he could give her the answer she wanted to hear, but he wasn't that heroic. "No."

She tossed the dandelion away. "You were blinded by mammon."

"Such an old-fashioned word, but yes, I suppose I was." His boots felt like they were dipped in lead. He considered his next words. He wouldn't share the details. She already thought he'd sold his soul to the devil. "I lost my friend Jacob."

She halted beside him, puzzled. "What are you saying, Gideon?"

His part in the death of his friend weighed heavily on him, pressing on his chest, making it hard to breathe. The tragedy had been the catalyst to facing who he'd become. "A terrible accident on the job took Jacob's life."

9

Fannie settled on the seat of the spring wagon. Covering a yawn, she adjusted her knit shawl against the cool morning air. An apricot streak on the horizon promised the sun's arrival wasn't far off.

They were on their way to the barn raising. With an hour-long drive ahead of them, she'd begun milking earlier than usual. She and Gideon had a morning routine in the barn that ran smoothly as long as the goats went along with the plan. Fortunately, they had cooperated today.

Looking out across the pasture cloaked in the half-light of early dawn, she saw Titus circling the field on a mission only he was privy to. The nannies browsed in the brush with the kids playing close by.

Leland had offered to come by at midday and check on the herd while Prudy napped. He thanked Fannie for a good reason to get out of the house and stretch his legs.

Gideon came out of the shed with Uncle Will's leather tool belt and handsaw. Aunt Susie had offered Gideon the use of her late husband's tools for this frolic, and he had gratefully accepted. He set them in the back of the wagon next to Fannie's tote bag and a box containing two sour cream spice cakes and an applesauce cake.

Fannie breathed in the damp scent of a new day as excitement quivered through her. She'd looked forward to this frolic since the bishop had announced it two weeks ago.

Samuel, Sarah, and the children had already left in their buggy. Aunt Susie and Aunt Lucy would follow soon. They had hired a driver to take them in a van along with other friends.

Wearing a straw hat and a short-sleeve shirt that matched the green in his eyes, Gideon stepped up into the wagon and took his seat. Today, Tommy pulled the wagon. He would cover the seven miles to the site in about an hour.

Fannie tucked her chin into her shawl and listened to the horse making his way steadily over the highway. She relaxed into the sway of the wagon. The miles disappeared beneath its wheels.

"I bought a buggy."

Gideon's statement caused Fannie to sit up straight.

"What?" Surely she'd heard incorrectly.

His face lit up like Micah's did when sharing a wonderful discovery. "I went to Martin's and found a buggy I like. It's used. He has a few repairs to make on it, but it's a good one, so I bought it."

"That's wonderful." Wonderful because a buggy meant a commitment. Wonderful because a buggy indicated Gideon's intentions to the community. Wonderful because maybe she could truly believe what he'd said since the day he arrived on the farm.

"I've spoken to Samuel about building a shed to house it."

Fannie's heart beat hard in her chest. "You did?"

"He said yes. I'll use the plans the bishop approved when Samuel built his work shed."

Heady with the wonder of his revelation, Fannie clutched the edge of the wagon seat to keep from floating off into the air. Reminding her silly self there were many obstacles still to overcome, she and Gideon talked about additional safety features for the buggy, horses, and harnesses. Having listened when Uncle Will or Samuel had talked about such things, she was pleased to be able to hold up her end of the conversation.

In what felt like no time at all, they were one in a long line of gray-top buggies all moving in the same direction. The sun spread its golden rays across the wide fields as, one by one, the buggies turned into the lane that led to the work site.

The timbers damaged in the fire had been hauled away and the foundation repaired in preparation for this day. A group of men had already assembled and were listening while the boss of the job explained the plan for the day.

Gideon stopped the buggy near a large tent erected on the grassy front lawn. Beneath it were rows of tables and folding chairs where the men would be served their large noon meal.

Fannie's heart skipped a beat when she took Gideon's hand and climbed from the wagon. He handed her the box of cakes and her tote bag. "Danke."

Returning her smile, he leaped back into the wagon, eager to join the crowd of men.

Cherishing the conversation they'd had on the ride, Fannie walked across the grass to the tent. Children, including Mary and Malachi, were playing games under the watchful eye of older girls.

The van carrying Aunt Susie, Aunt Lucy, and other elderly members of the community drove into the yard and stopped in the driveway. Her aunts and two other ladies got out carrying baskets filled with food. A man stooped with age got out carrying his tool belt.

Placing her cakes on the dessert table, Fannie joined the women gathered in a circle beneath the tent. They were in the process of peeling potatoes. She took the seat next to Bonnie Esh. The bishop's wife introduced Fannie to Naomi King, Bonnie's cousin from a neighboring church district.

"We don't get to see each other as often as we'd like." Bonnie beamed at her cousin, a plump woman with a quick smile and dimples.

On the opposite side of the circle, Sarah chatted with a friend who was also pregnant.

The hum of a generator, the pounding cacophony of many hammers, and the *ka-chunk ka-chunk* of a nail gun created the background noise that accompanied the women's conversations.

"Hi, Fannie." Rachel Stoltzfus plopped into the chair next to her with a groan. "It feels good to sit." She brushed a hand across her damp brow. "We're rotating helpers at the stove."

Arriving prepared to work, Fannie pulled her vegetable peeler from her tote. By noon the crowd would be hungry. The women needed to prepare a lot of food to feed the men and their families.

"Have your goats escaped again?" Rachel dropped a peeled potato in a bucket of cold water and took another.

"No. We haven't had any more trouble." Making short work of her spud, Fannie dropped it into the same bucket. "I still believe it was just young people out creating mischief."

Rachel dug an eye from her potato. "I saw Gideon drop you off at the house. He seems nice."

Fannie ignored Sarah's indelicate snort. "He worked in construction for years and has been a big help on the farm." She hoped she would catch an occasional glimpse of him among the men swarming across the site while she helped with the meal preparations. Perhaps at the noon meal she would have an opportunity to speak to him.

Leah Schrock, the bride-to-be, brushed a stray potato skin from her apron. "Is he coming back to be baptized into the church?"

Sarah *tsked*. "I have my doubts."

Her statement created a stir among the women.

Sarah looked up from the potato she was furiously stripping of its skin. "We were in the same crowd as kids running around." She let that statement hang in the air before adding, "I'm sure he hasn't told Fannie much about *that* time in his life."

A low murmur rippled through the circle of women as they

exchanged comments and opinions. "I imagine he owned a car."

"Do you suppose he sold it before coming back?"

"Do you think he has things in a storage unit like the ones out on the highway? The English always have more things than they need."

Fannie gripped her peeler until her knuckles turned white. "He stopped at Martin's and ordered a buggy."

Her heated words silenced everyone for a moment before a flurry of whispers hissed through the gathering. Heat climbing her neck, Fannie tossed her potato into the water. She brushed her fingers across her cheek, shocked that she'd spoken out in this group of ladies, many of whom she did not know.

"He likes my rhubarb-raisin pie," said Bonnie.

The conversation ceased, and along with it, any speculation concerning Gideon.

Bonnie winked at Fannie.

With those few words Bonnie had made it clear Gideon had visited her husband, the bishop. A bishop's wife did not share private information, but Bonnie had found a roundabout way to say it and stop the conjecture.

Fannie picked up the bucket of peeled potatoes and hurried to the kitchen. She didn't know herself anymore. Her outburst had been out of character. Where had such boldness come from?

Entering the kitchen, she greeted her aunts, busy at the stove stirring saucepans of chicken gravy. The mouthwatering scent of chicken baking in the oven filled the room. Women were dredging more pieces in eggs and seasoned bread crumbs, and placing them in aluminum pans. The hostess, a large woman, carefully orchestrated the prep work and the shuffling of baked chicken in and out of the oven. At the kitchen table, teenage girls tore bread into small chunks and chopped celery and onions for the bread dressing.

The hostess, her face pink from the heat of the kitchen, appeared at Fannie's side. "Bring those potatoes out here onto the porch."

Fannie followed her through a side door to an airy porch occupied by a summer kitchen. Another batch of chicken baked in this second oven. The pots on the burners were partially filled with bubbling water. The hostess slipped the potatoes into one.

"Here's a few more." Sarah had followed Fannie.

Fannie stepped away from the stove to make room for Sarah. Without looking back, she slipped through the crowded kitchen to the back door, hoping to avoid her cousin's sharp tongue. But she wasn't quick enough. Having sat all morning, first in the buggy, and afterward peeling potatoes, her hip and leg ached.

"Fannie." Sarah grasped her arm and pulled her to a stop at the bottom of the kitchen steps.

Refusing to look at her cousin, Fannie stared at the work site. The sharp crack of hammers hitting nails reverberated through the air. Tiny particles of sawdust floated by on the breeze.

"You know how unhappy I am about Gideon's return." Sarah's words were an annoying murmur in Fannie's ear.

Fannie pulled away from Sarah and crossed her arms. Hope and doubt were constantly fighting for the upper hand in her thoughts about Gideon. Sarah's words had rung with the hard truth—Gideon hadn't told her anything about his running-around years.

"He's no longer that boy. He knows what he wants now." She wasn't about to share the knowledge that he still had questions.

Young girls brushed by carrying stacks of dinner plates.

Fannie held the door for others carrying tumblers and flatware.

Sarah threw up her hands. "I don't know what else I can say to warn you away." She turned to face the site.

Micah and his friends stood in the center of the new floor and watched Samuel's team measure and nail together the framework that would be raised into place.

Sarah glared at the men. "At the Grossdawdi Haus yesterday, Gideon was oiling a leather tool belt. Was that Daed's belt?"

"Yes." Fannie tried to find Gideon among the men. "Why?"

"Did Mamm say he could use it?"

Fannie nodded. "Aunt Susie is pleased Uncle Will's tools are being used again."

Sarah shook her head. "Am I the only one who can see this is going to end in disaster?" She turned to Fannie. "Let me be blunt."

I thought you were already doing that.

"Look at you, Fannie." Sarah swept her hand through the air, taking in Fannie's height and breadth. "While away, he has met English women. You can't compete with them."

Fannie's breath caught in her throat. Her heart shriveled in her chest.

A pitying pout on her lips, Sarah patted Fannie's arm. "Don't fall for his pretty words. And don't let Mamm and Aunt Lucy push you into anything." She returned to the circle of woman peeling potatoes.

Fannie tried to find Gideon among the men.

His desire to return to Winsome and to live plain was a difficult process for him. She hoped he didn't regret the choice he made in the end. He'd come to mean so much to her. She'd been so sure she could keep a distance between them. An emotional distance if not a physical one. But her heart had paid no heed, and now she wanted desperately for him to stay.

Could she accept Gideon for who he was—his past as well as his present? There were so many shades to the man's character. He had knowledge of things she knew nothing about. He intrigued her. He struggled to reconcile the two very different cultures that had become a part of him and how he viewed the world.

Fannie touched her scar. Was Sarah right? Was she too boring to hold Gideon's interest?

Jostled from her woolgathering by a young girl carrying plates of butter to set out, Fannie went to help finish setting the tables for the first sitting. The mismatched plates from local thrift shops made a colorful table.

Next, she helped set out salt and pepper shakers, side dishes of pickles and relishes, and coolers filled to the brim with lemonade, iced tea, and water.

Emotional turmoil didn't stop Fannie from appreciating how easily the meal came together when everyone pitched in and helped.

The men were doing the same thing, only on a grander scale. Where a short time ago there had been nothing but a foundation, there was now the skeleton framework of a barn.

Helping each other made rebuilding the barn possible. She should consider taking a lesson from today. Gideon wanted to rebuild his life here among the people. What had she done to help him with that? Taking up a handful of forks, she set one at each plate. Gideon wasn't the only one with a great deal to consider.

10

The man in charge of the barn raising stood on the new floorboards. Taking a deep breath, he bellowed a command in German.

Muscles straining, Gideon added his strength to that of the men around him and pushed up on his beam. Other men pulled on ropes. In one sweeping motion, the first beam was lifted high into the air. On either side, teams of men moved in to lift framed sections of the barn's sides and then secure them to the flooring and framework.

Relieved to have a short break, Gideon walked to the table holding drinks, hoping to catch a glimpse of Fannie. He poured a glass of water from the tall, insulated cooler.

All morning, the frame of the barn had risen piece by piece against the deep blue of the sky. The younger, nimbler members of the crew worked high in the crisscrossing timbers that would soon hold the roof. The older men framed the doors and windows, or preset nails in the lumber that would be used for the barn's siding. The littlest boys were busy collecting scraps of waste wood and making a pile off to one side, where it was in no one's way.

"Looks good, jah?" Brian Fisher approached and stood beside Gideon.

Holding his straw hat in his hand, Gideon finished drinking his water. "Amazing. I am always awestruck by what this community can accomplish by working together."

He stood quiet for a moment watching the work. Each man on the site knew where he needed to be and what task he had to do as the building progressed.

Earlier in the week, the local lumber company had dropped off pallets of lumber in the level pasture alongside the driveway. The younger, less experienced boys had the job of transporting the lumber from the pasture to the building site where space was at a premium.

"Are you still looking for a horse?" Brian helped himself to a glass of water.

"I am." He had ordered the buggy, now he needed the horse to pull it. "Thought I'd go to the next auction."

"John Zimmerman brought a sorrel along for his nephew, but it seems the boy has his heart set on a different horse. Would you like to take a look at the sorrel before leaving?"

"Absolutely." Gideon was pleased Brian had thought to ask him.

From his vantage point on the ground, Gideon could see Abram high on the peak of the barn. His brother had done a clever job of avoiding him. No matter where Gideon happened to be, Abram was sure to be someplace else. The ache of disappointment lurked beneath the joy of being a part of the community helping one of their own. But Abram's cold shoulder wasn't the only burden he carried today.

He turned to Brian and asked, "Is Hiram King here?"

Brian pointed to the spot where the boards were being premeasured and cut. "He's the big man with the streak of silver down the center of his beard." He looked in the direction of the food tents. "I saw his wife with the women when I let Ava and the children off at the house."

With over a hundred men in attendance, Gideon had his work cut out catching up with the man. Right now, it was enough to know he was here. "I have to speak with him before the day is out."

Taking another glass of water, Gideon turned his attention to the tents where the women worked. He searched the crowd for Fannie and found her walking around the tables helping to prepare them for the first seating for lunch.

Hoping she would look up from her task and see him, he lingered a moment longer. A little bit at a time she was shedding her protective shell. The Sunday he'd given her the choice whether or not to walk with him to church had been a turning point for her. He'd been pleased when she took the risk and said yes.

As if she sensed him watching her, her gaze met his and she smiled. His heart tripped.

Why she hadn't already been snapped up by one of the local boys bewildered him. She had so much to offer. She was kind, gentle, and a good listener. He should know. She willingly listened to him as he figured out his reentry into the life of an Amish man.

Drinking the last of the water from his tumbler, he shoved his hat back onto his head and prepared to go back to work.

On a ladder propped against the bare wall studs, Gideon reached down and took a wide board from the man below him. Hoisting it up, he waited for Brian to take the other end. Together they positioned the board and nailed it in place.

With a quick swipe of his thumb, Gideon confirmed the set of the nail head in the wood. He felt deep satisfaction being with the men of the community and applying his skills to help. Today, he'd also reconnected with more friends from his youth. Like church Sunday, greetings had been reserved, but he never felt unwelcome.

The ladies had begun to serve the noon meal in shifts. When the time came for the crew Gideon worked with to sit down to the meal, he left his straw hat and tool belt on the new barn floor and headed for the tent. He had to dodge around the empty lumber wagon when it rattled by filled with boys.

Beneath the tent, teenage girls were gathering up the dirty dishes left by the previous shift and replacing them with clean place settings. Finding a seat next to Brian, Gideon sat quietly, trying to remember the last time he'd felt so content.

The women set out platters piled high with chicken followed by bowls of mashed potatoes, gravy, and dressing. The prettiest girl at the frolic was setting baskets of rolls on the tables. Fannie.

She looked at him, and Gideon's heart danced a jig behind his ribs. Thankfully, no one could see the phenomenon. Dancing was forbidden.

Fannie placed one basket on the table closest to the kitchen, then walked straight up to him and handed him the other basket, a hesitant smile on her lips.

Puzzled, Gideon smiled wide, leaving no room for doubt that he was glad to see her.

Her smile brightened and grew bolder, as he'd hoped it would.

"How are you doing up there?" she whispered and glanced about as if she was afraid to be caught talking to him.

"Keeping up." He hadn't meant to sound so rueful, but there it was. He'd softened over the years. "Good thing I've had a few weeks doing barn work. Otherwise, I'd be on the ground with the elders presetting nails."

She laughed and hurried back to the kitchen. Before stepping out of sight, she cast one last glance over her shoulder at him.

He imagined what it would be like to have her sitting at his side. In a society where there were definite gender roles, Fannie sitting at a table of men would never happen, especially if it meant shirking duties in the kitchen. On a day like today, everyone did their fair share of the work.

The talk among the men slowed to an occasional murmur as they dug into the delicious food. Eager to get back to work, the men concentrated on eating.

The tender and juicy baked chicken fell off the bones. The flaky roll melted in Gideon's mouth. To produce a meal this good for a crowd this size took the same precision and organization in the kitchen as building the barn.

Gideon sopped up the last of the chicken gravy with his dinner roll and popped it in his mouth. He watched the lumber wagon roll by. The horses pulling it were a well-trained team. Boys walked along on either side of the wagon to help unload the lumber closer to where it would be used. Gideon paused and looked again. The boards weren't properly secured.

A shiver shot up his spine as he rose to his feet. He trotted toward the wagon. Taking this load into the close quarters near the barn's foundation could end in disaster.

Picking up his pace, he brushed past an old-timer with a snowy beard and wire-framed glasses. He called out to the boy on the wagon seat, "Hold up."

A boy walking beside the wagon looked Gideon's way.

The squeal of slipping boards filled the air.

The boy looked up and froze as the lumber shifted with a groan.

Gideon dove for him. His teeth clacked together, and his elbow burned across the gravel. He held on to the boy as they fell hard to the ground. The boy grunted when Gideon landed on top of him. Holding him in a viselike grip, Gideon rolled away from the wagon—away from the danger.

Eyes closed, Gideon's ears were filled with the rumble of shifting, sliding, toppling lumber. Choking on the dirt kicked up by the boards, he tensed, expecting to feel crushing pain as they struck his back and hips. Miraculously, the pain didn't come. Over the pounding of his heart and his labored breathing, he heard screams and shouts.

Dazed, Gideon lurched off the boy and onto his knees. He kneeled there, gasping and coughing, trying to clear the dust from his throat. He looked over at the boy.

The kid's eyes were too big for his pale face. Tears had made muddy streaks in the dust on his cheeks as he struggled to catch the breath that Gideon had knocked out of him, but he seemed unhurt.

Men crowded around them, talking and gesturing.

His line of vision blocked by the legs of the men reaching to help him, Gideon lost sight of the boy. Bending double, he gave into the trembling that had taken over his body. Staying on his knees, he thanked God for the good fortune of being in the right place at the right time.

11

Fannie set a basket of rolls on the table. The basket would be empty with one pass. The men were thick as locusts beneath the tent and just as hungry. They devoured every morsel of food set before them with gusto.

Taking a moment to speak with Gideon had made her forget about the ache in her hip. He'd taken his hat off, and his hair stood on end like shocks of corn at harvest. Her attention continued to stray to the end of the table where he sat. She couldn't help herself. She liked looking at him.

She was startled when he jumped up, his face taut and pale beneath his tan.

She paused in her work. Was he ill? He'd looked fine a few minutes ago when she spoke to him. She started to go to him, hoping he hadn't gotten heatstroke working in the sun for so many hours.

He dashed from the tent, his hand in the air, trying to get someone's attention on the wagon. The team of horses looked like they were doing fine in the hands of the boy sitting on the wagon seat.

A terrible sound rent the air.

In horror, Fannie watched the boards on the wagon shift and roll. Rumbling and squealing, they fell off the wagon.

Her heart in her throat, she watched Gideon run straight toward the avalanche of lumber.

Fannie screamed. Her heart burned painfully as she watched Gideon dive for the boy. Jostled by men leaping up from the tables, she stumbled and caught herself on the chairs. Sobbing, she moved with the crowd. Fear held her in its terrible grip.

Gideon had surely been crushed to death.

She cried out to God, "Don't let him die. Please don't let him die." She fought her way through the crowd, tears blurring her vision, as she cried, "Gideon!"

Men held the bridles of the frightened horses. Like a giant game of pick-up sticks, boards lay in a massive jumble on the ground. Others rested half on and half off the tilted wagon bed.

Fannie shoved through the wall of solid-colored shirts and suspenders. "Please."

One of the men took pity on her and called out, helping to open a path for her.

Gideon lay on the ground.

Fannie's stomach turned. Ends of boards had dug into the ground only inches from him.

Then he moved.

Someone tried to hold her back. In the haze of terror, she heard voices say, "Too dangerous."

"Let the men clear the boards."

"We'll bring him to the tent."

Throwing off the restraining hands, she reached his side and fell to the ground beside him.

He was on his knees and bent double.

Fannie sobbed and tears flowed, blurring her vision. She wanted to fling her arms around him, but feared hurting him. "Gideon." Ignoring the men on all sides, she placed her hand on his back.

He wheezed, fighting to catch his breath.

"Are you hurt?" Dust caught in the back of her throat. She touched his arm, feeling the warmth of him with her shaking hand. Her heart burst with relief. Tears flowed freely from her eyes.

He rubbed a hand over his face. "I think I'm okay." He didn't sound all that sure. His voice sounded thin from the shock of what had happened. He looked down at his arms and legs as though checking for injuries. "I think I'm all right."

Someone jostled Fannie, but she refused to budge. "That's *gut*." She was becoming a master of the understatement where this man was concerned. Something inside her snapped, and she gave into the urge to put her arm around his shoulder.

He turned and wrapped an arm around her.

She clung to him and burst into a fresh round of tears. "I thought I'd lost you." She held on to him and cried.

His arm tightened around her as if he could absorb her fear.

Pulling out of the awkward hug, Fannie rubbed her face with the sleeve of her dress. "You're bleeding."

He'd scraped the skin on his arm. Pieces of gravel were embedded in the wound.

Samuel and a man with a first-aid kit crouched on the other side of Gideon. They asked him questions, trying to assess his injuries.

Fannie wanted more than anything to remain at his side, but other men nudged her aside so they could help Gideon.

Her vision blurry with tears and her arms and legs trembling, she'd be of little assistance to him. Still on her knees, she scooted back.

Someone helped her to her feet.

She lost more ground when the men moved around her inspecting the wagon and looking at the lumber. Standing on tiptoe, she tried to see around broad shoulders and wide-brimmed hats, but was unsuccessful.

A cry arose behind Fannie. A knot of women bore down on the men. Leading the pack was the nice lady she'd met just this morning—Naomi King, Bonnie Esh's cousin.

"Where is he?"

The men parted for Naomi and her entourage. Seeing an opportunity to get another glimpse of Gideon, Fannie moved with them.

Reaching the edge of the crowd, Fannie's heart sank.

Gideon was no longer there.

She tried to locate him, but hemmed in on all sides, she couldn't move.

Naomi dropped to her knees beside the boy. "Ben." She pulled the boy into her arms and wept into his hair.

He wiggled away from her embrace. "I'm okay, Mamm. Just out of breath from being knocked out of the way." He wiped a shaking hand down his face. The heels of his hands were skinned raw where he'd tried to break his unexpected fall. "My hands sting is all." He looked up at the man standing behind Naomi. "Daed."

His father, a big man, helped him to his feet. "Can you walk, son?"

"Jah."

The young boy's legs looked rubbery, but his father and another man stepped in to help lead him to the tent. His mother followed. Remaining within the cluster of women, Fannie moved along with them.

Joy brimmed in Fannie's heart and eyes when she got beyond the crowd and spied Gideon seated beneath the tent drinking a glass of lemonade. Samuel stood at his side.

Fannie sat in the chair next to him. She had to either sit or fall down. She felt physically weak and emotionally wrung out. "Can I get you anything?" Embarrassed by her terrified response earlier, she kept her chin down, looking at him from beneath her lashes.

His lips bent in a weak imitation of his usual crooked grin. "No, thank you."

She wanted to touch him again, but cool logic had returned. She looked away.

Samuel put his hat on. He looked at first at Fannie, and then at

Gideon. "You should take it easy this afternoon."

Fannie's gaze followed Samuel when he left the shade of the tent and walked into the sunshine. He had seen her fall apart and hug Gideon. He would surely report the incident to Sarah.

The touch of Gideon's fingers as he took her hand sent tingling waves of warmth through Fannie. She looked down at their interlaced fingers, then lifted her face to look at him.

The gentleness in his smile squeezed more tears from her stinging eyes. "I'm so glad you're alive." Her voice broke on that last word.

"Me too." He squeezed her hand. "Me too."

"Where is he? Gideon Zook? *There* you are." Aunt Lucy moved between the tables, arms pumping as if functioning on a full head of steam.

Aunt Susie hurried along in her wake, huffing and puffing.

Bearing down on Gideon with the look of women on a mission, the aunts didn't stop for man, woman, or child. Everyone stepped out of their way.

Aunt Lucy saw the bandage Samuel had applied around his arm. "Oh, are you hurt?" Her eyes held a glint of—was that excitement? She took his hand and stared at the white gauze, as if she could see through the layers.

Gideon mouthed at Fannie, "Bloodthirsty woman."

She bit her lip. If she started to laugh, she wouldn't be able to stop and Aunt Lucy would be treating her for hysterics.

"Are you bruised? I can make a poultice for bruises. Heals them up quicker than quick." She pinched the short sleeve of his shirt between her fingers. "Where are they? You can't have a fall like that and not have a bruise."

"Ach. Do stop, Lucy." Exasperated, Aunt Susie sank into a chair. "The boy isn't going to show you his bruises here in the tent."

Gideon looked at Fannie with alarm in his eyes and whispered,

"This 'boy' isn't going to show her his bruises here or anywhere else."

This time Fannie covered her mouth and pretended to have a coughing fit to hide her laughter.

"All right, then." Aunt Lucy backed off a smidge. "I can always make the poultice, and you can put it on yourself." She leaned in again. "Hematomas. Big ones. You have to be careful with them, ya know."

Fannie bit her bottom lip.

Gideon looked at her and narrowed his eyes, making it harder for her to hold in the laughter.

Aunt Susie patted his other hand. "I was so afraid when we heard what had happened. Seeing you sitting here . . ." She looked at Fannie and raised her eyebrows before looking back at Gideon. "It does my heart good." She whacked her heavily veined hands to her thighs. "That's all. Fannie, you take care of our boy."

Fannie squeaked. When had Gideon become "our boy"? *Mercy!*

Standing, Susie touched Lucy's shoulder. "Let's go, sister. Back to the kitchen. The youngsters are fine."

A look of disappointment passed over Aunt Lucy's face. Her eyes darted between Fannie and Gideon before landing on their entwined hands. Her eyes grew round, and the disappointment gave way to a speculative gleam. She turned and hurried after Susie, her words floating back to Fannie. "Do you suppose what happened has done the trick?"

The heat of a blush traveled up Fannie's neck and cheeks. Her aunts were incorrigible.

"Hey." Gideon gently shook their linked hands. "Look at me."

Fannie glanced up at him, skimming her other hand across her scar.

"First, I want to know what this poultice involves. Is it herbal? Is there something gross in it like ground chicken feet? Will it make my skin slough off?"

Giggling, Fannie shook her head. Before she could say anything, Gideon continued.

"And second," his voice dropped to a whisper, "I don't know what you might think about this, but maybe, looking into the future, when I'm a member of the church," he gestured toward the wagon and the men around it, "all this really did do the trick."

Fannie's heart thundered in her ears. Was he saying what she thought he was saying? Shocked by his words, she couldn't think properly. Clinging to his hand, she stared into his green eyes, overwhelmed by the promise she saw there.

He raised his eyebrows, as though he expected her to comment.

She shook her head. "You are in shock. I think you hit your head and have no idea what you're saying."

He exhaled with a huff and rubbed his free hand across his mouth. "Happy I got there in time." He glanced over at the boy being helped to a chair close by.

Relieved he didn't say any more about his previous statement, Fannie said, "Everyone is glad you saw what was happening."

He glanced toward the barn, taking shape beneath the hands of many workers. "I think my legs are too shaky to go back up there." He watched the men around the wagon. They were inspecting it and the lumber for damage. "Maybe I can help from the ground."

"*Maybe* you need to sit for a minute." Fannie looked down. When had she become so forward with this man? She peeped at him from beneath her lashes.

He watched her without a hint of disapproval.

She glanced up at the new group of men entering the tent without hats or tool belts. "I have to go serve." She leaned against his shoulder, feeling like she was abandoning him.

As though he read her mind, he raised her hand and brushed his lips across the back of it. "Go ahead. I'm okay."

Fannie sat. And sat. Shock rooted her to the chair.

Gideon smiled a secret little smile. "Go. You have work to do. Jah?"

"Jah." She whispered agreement. Anything else required thought.

"You going to be okay?" His voice was a tender murmur.

"Jah." She looked away—she had to in order to think. "D-Don't climb any ladders." Heat raced up her cheeks. She put her hand to her scar. "Please."

Gideon reached up and gently took her hand away from her face. He held it tight. "Don't hide behind your hand. Not with me. Not ever. You're beautiful, Fannie."

Fannie's heart fluttered. Beautiful? She looked at him, shaking her head in disbelief.

He squeezed her hand and whispered. "I did not bump my head, and I know exactly what I'm saying."

His crooked smile melted Fannie's heart. She blinked hard to hold the tears at bay, but one escaped.

Gideon wiped it away with the pad of his thumb. "I'll stay off the ladder. Promise."

She didn't want to leave him. The current of longing that now flowed through her was stronger than anything she'd ever experienced. "Danke." Standing, she fled for the safety of the kitchen.

Gideon watched Fannie weave her way through the tables filling up with the next team of hungry men. Drawing in a deep breath, he wiped his arm across his brow. Had he miscalculated the distance or been a few seconds too slow, he and the boy would have been crushed beneath the wood.

The adrenaline that had carried him through the heroic effort was subsiding. Soon he'd feel as limp as a well-used rag. Closing his eyes, he bowed his head and offered up thanks for two lives spared in the accident.

Feeling the presence of another person, Gideon looked up. Jacob's father, Hiram King—the man he needed to speak with—stood in front of him. Gideon sat up straight as Hiram swung a chair around to sit facing him.

Jacob's father dropped into the chair. His skin had an underlying gray cast not covered by his suntan. His eyes held a dark, wounded expression. Gideon's heart thumped hard. Why had this man sought him out? Did he already know who Gideon was?

"I'm Hiram King." The big man ran his hand down his full beard.

All Gideon's carefully rehearsed words were buried deep beneath the physical and emotional fallout of all that had taken place at the wagon and with Fannie. He sat dumb before this big man with the sad face.

Hiram cleared his throat. "Danke." He swallowed hard. "For saving Benjamin's life. He's my youngest son."

Gideon's heart jumped and pounded so hard it hurt. *Son?* He glanced at the boy. He sat with his friends and a woman.

He had to concentrate to think through the connections. Benjamin was Hiram's *son*. That meant the boy he'd saved was Jacob's *brother*. Gideon's gaze darted between the man and the boy.

The woman with Benjamin rose, leaving him to his friends, and came to sit beside Hiram.

"This is my wife, Naomi." Hiram took her hand in his. "*We* thank you for what you did."

Wiping tears from her eyes, Naomi's voice was nothing more than a ragged whisper. "Jah." Her hand covered her mouth in an attempt to stifle a sob. "We couldn't bear to lose another son."

Gideon's stomach rolled, threatening to toss up the heavy chicken dinner he'd eaten. If he didn't say what he had to say this instant, he feared he never would. Clearing the knot of fear and trepidation from his throat, he shook his head. "I don't deserve your thanks."

He raised his hand and silenced their automatic protests. "Please, hear me out." First he had to be sure beyond a doubt that these people were the mother and father of the man who had been like a brother to him. "Did you have an older son? Jacob King?"

"Jah."

"He moved to the city and worked in construction?"

"Jah. Jah. He chose to leave the settlement." The wide-eyed terror from nearly losing Benjamin merged with a glimmer of curiosity.

Gideon held Hiram's gaze with his own. "You lost him in an accident." His voice broke on the last word.

Hiram nodded. "The company he worked for demolished old buildings." He frowned. "On the last job, a wall fell on him." He looked over his shoulder at Benjamin. "How is it possible I nearly lost another son in such a way?" He turned his attention back to Gideon. "You were friends with our Jacob?"

"Good friends." He tightened his mouth to stop his lips from trembling. "My name is Gideon Zook. I was there at the accident."

Naomi gasped and reached for Gideon's hand. "Tell us. How did it happen?"

Focusing on the strength of her hand squeezing his, Gideon denied himself the solace of tears. He wanted to look any place except at the faces of this man and this woman. He didn't want to see their pain. He didn't want to see the horror in their expressions when he told them what he'd done.

But he had to do this. He deserved to bear the brunt of their anger. They deserved the truth. "I drove the excavator." He took a deep breath and spoke quickly before he could change his mind. "I demolished the wall that came down on Jacob." His voice gave out. Only a whisper was left in him. "I killed him. I'm sorry."

He could no longer keep the anguish inside. He pressed his fingers to his eyes in an effort to hold back the tears. He tightened the muscles in his shoulders, but nothing could stop the shaking. He fought to hold back the sob building in his chest. In the last few minutes, Jacob's death had gotten all tied up with what had happened with Benjamin. The turmoil inside him spilled over in hot tears.

A gentle hand rubbed across his shoulder. "Surely there were rules about safety." Naomi's voice held no condemnation, only the desire to understand.

Gideon nodded. "For some reason, he stepped closer to the wall." The words came out in a tortured rush. "I didn't see him until it was too late." He shook his head. "I'm so sorry."

Minutes passed, the silence finally broken by Hiram's voice raspy from tears. "Jacob's death was an accident. Though there is nothing to forgive, I know you feel there is." He placed his calloused hand over Gideon's fisted hands. "We forgive you. We don't blame you for Jacob's death, and we are so grateful to you for saving Benjamin's life."

The tight band of muscle constricting Gideon's breathing to ragged bursts of air, loosened. The sharp edges of self-condemnation dulled.

Hiram shuffled his feet. "We're glad we know." He patted Naomi's hand. "Today we saw God's presence when Benjamin could have been taken from us. We know God was present at Jacob's death too." He cleared his throat. "We don't question God's ways."

Clutching her husband's hand, Naomi nodded her agreement.

Under the gaze of the stalwart man holding his emotions in check, Gideon felt like a blubbering baby. Had the man's staid acceptance come with age or many losses?

The heavy darkness Gideon had carried for so long began to melt beneath the warm glow of forgiveness. The relief was almost too much to bear.

For the next hour, while hungry men entered the tent, ate their fill and hurried back to work, Gideon shared many memories about his friendship with Jacob. Hiram, Naomi, and young Ben were eager to hear everything he remembered. The time with them helped to begin the healing of Gideon's heart. The relief that they knew and did not condemn him uncoiled the tension in his chest. He could breathe so deeply, he felt light-headed.

When the time came to return to work, Hiram stood and enveloped Gideon in a strong hug. "You'll come visit us soon, jah?"

"Jah," Gideon agreed as Naomi pulled him close for a hug.

Someone had found Gideon's hat and set it on the table behind him. Placing it on his head, he looked up. Fannie was beneath the tents, helping to clear the dirty dishes.

She glanced up and stopped, caught in Gideon's gaze. She looked at Hiram, Naomi, and young Ben leaving the tent, and her gaze came back to rest on Gideon.

He smiled and turned to go back to work. What Fannie saw today was only half the story. One day soon he would finish telling her the truth about Jacob.

The rest of the afternoon, Gideon worked on the ground handing boards up to Brian. Brian, in turn, handed the boards up into the rafters where a floor was being laid for hay storage. Lifting one board at a time took all of Gideon's strength. He also wasn't setting any records doing it, but no one seemed to mind.

The men that had been withdrawn earlier now attempted to engage him in conversation. His willingness to put himself in harm's way had broken through the reservations others had had about him.

He wouldn't recommend the method to anyone, but he certainly appreciated the results.

The late-afternoon sun shone brightly on the new barn standing tall and solid against the backdrop of emerald cornfields and deep-blue sky.

Gideon helped Fannie into the wagon before climbing in next to her.

She sighed. "It's magnificent."

Gideon looked at her and smiled. "Is that pride I hear in your voice?"

She blushed and looked down at her hands before nudging him with her shoulder. "Not for myself. For our community and the way everyone pulled together to help someone in need."

"I see. There are occasions when a little pride is okay?" So much good had happened today that he felt lighthearted and couldn't help but tease her.

A smug little smile flitted across her lips. "Tell me you don't feel pride having helped."

She had him there. He did feel pride, and a great deal of satisfaction.

A frown creased her brow. "You're feeling ok?"

"Jah. I'm fine."

Her cheeks grew pink, and she looked away.

The memory of what had happened between them earlier had not been far from his thoughts all afternoon.

With a click of his tongue he got Tommy moving.

There was an instant of resistance before the wagon moved forward.

Fannie looked over her shoulder at the horse tied to the rear of the wagon. "We're leaving the frolic with an extra horse."

"Wondered if you'd noticed."

"She's a beautiful sorrel. Now, are you going to tell me how that happened, or do I have to start guessing?"

He could see she enjoyed the teasing as much as he did. Eager to share his tale of good fortune, he said, "Fannie, meet Fiona. Fiona, this is Fannie."

Fannie feigned a regal air. "How do you do, Fiona?"

Gideon grinned. "She's sound and has an even temperament. Not the fastest, but safe." *Safe for Fannie to drive.*

The thought zinged so fast through Gideon's mind, he jerked in his seat. He felt Fannie's gaze on him, but he chose not to look at her for fear she would see something in his expression and ask for an explanation. Right now, he had no answers.

Had he chosen this horse with her in mind, even subconsciously? He hadn't thought about it, but the mind could play tricks on a person. And after the day he'd had, he wasn't certain he fully understood himself.

Over the course of ten hours, so much had changed. He needed time to think when he wasn't so physically tired or emotionally wrung out. There was one thing he was absolutely certain of, though. He was right where he wanted to be—sitting next to Fannie.

12

Fannie raised her window shade and breathed in the fresh early morning air. The sun touched the tops of the trees with its yellow light.

In the next bedroom, Aunt Susie stirred. She'd wake Aunt Lucy, and soon they would be preparing breakfast.

Treading softly down the stairs, Fannie stopped at the back door to slip into her barn shoes. She left the kitchen door open, latching the screen door behind her. The bells on the nanny goats rang close as they gathered for their morning milking. Inside the barn, the kids protested their confinement to the weaning pen.

The week since the barn raising had passed in a blur of activity. A new shed for Gideon's buggy and tack had been completed two days ago. The men had worked hard to have it built in time for yesterday when Gideon brought his buggy home.

Fannie had wanted to accompany him and Samuel into town, but Gideon had insisted she stay until he knew Fiona was steady in traffic.

Fannie had waited impatiently for him. The moment she heard the sound of Fiona coming up the lane, she'd left the garden and run to meet him. Fiona had the beautiful gait of a trotter, lifting her feet high. Her mane flew about her neck, and her nostrils flared as if she knew this was a special moment.

Now, hurrying across the dewy grass toward the barn, Fannie imagined a window box on the shed overflowing with a full wave of pink and purple petunias. She wanted to plant a small garden along the side of it, as well. Aunt Susie would help her choose perennials to transplant from the established flower beds.

Looking in the direction of the shed, she paused in her musing. Something large and white lay on the grass close to the shed. Indistinct in the early light, she couldn't imagine what it could be. There hadn't been a wind through the night strong enough to blow something that large around the yard.

Fannie hurried closer. Her heart sped up as she realized the white lump wasn't debris at all. It had fur.

Titus!

One leg and a large paw twitched. Running the last few steps, Fannie dropped to her knees. "Titus. What happened?" A puddle of vomit soaked the grass nearby.

His eyes seemed to plead for help.

"Gideon!" Fannie screamed. Her heart pounded so hard it deafened her. Wanting to comfort her dog, she ran her hand over his side and down his legs, at the same time looking for any injuries. "Gideon!" She blinked back her tears.

"Fannie, what is it?" Gideon ran toward her, pitchfork in hand.

The screen door on the house slammed as her aunts flew out onto the porch and down the steps toward her.

"He's sick." Seeing her strong herd guardian unable lift his head or stand frightened her.

The dog labored to breathe.

"Hey, fella. What's the matter?" His voice soothing, Gideon kneeled next to Fannie and ran gentle hands along Titus's stomach and chest.

He shook his head. "I'm not finding any injuries." He looked at the puddle in the grass. "That's not kibble. Looks like raw meat."

Fannie shook her head. "I don't feed him meat."

"Something poisoned his system. He's having a hard time breathing."

She stroked Titus, crooning to him. "Good boy. It's gonna be okay." His ears were cold to her touch.

Gideon stood and spoke to Aunt Susie. "We need an old blanket to put him on and something to hold a sample of what he threw up. I'll run over to Leland's and call the vet. Let him know we're coming." He took off running and disappeared on the lane through the cornfield.

Aunt Susie brought a blanket out of the house.

With Aunt Lucy's help, Fannie lifted Titus onto the blanket, moving first his front quarters followed by his rear. Sitting at his side waiting for Gideon to return, Fannie talked to the unresponsive dog and fought the panic rising inside her. The rattle of Leland's pickup truck approaching the house brought her to her feet.

Moving quickly, Leland and Gideon loaded Titus into the bed of the truck.

Fannie started to climb in beside him, but Gideon's hand clamped around her arm. "You'll ride in the cab." His hard voice allowed for no argument. He helped her into the truck before leaping into the back with Titus.

Fannie buckled her seat belt. Twisting around, she looked through the cab window, willing Titus to keep fighting and praying he'd be okay.

Doc Silva had his office open when they arrived. Though unshaven and sporting bedhead, he was alert and in command of the situation.

Gideon and Leland carried Titus into the examination room. Fannie followed, ready to stay with her faithful herd guardian.

Gideon caught her sleeve. "Fannie, come sit with me in the waiting room. Let Doc do his job."

She leaned over Titus and ran her hand through the warm fur covering his thick neck. Her tears dropped onto his fur as she whispered into the big dog's ear, "You get well, you hear me? The nannies need you. I need you." Sniffing, she let Gideon lead her from the room. She sank onto the wooden bench attached to the wall of the waiting room.

Hot tears stung her eyes. "What if he doesn't make it?"

Gideon slid closer and wrapped both arms around her. "He's healthy and strong. We have to believe he'll be all right."

Leaning into his strength, Fannie let the tears flow down her cheeks. Sharing her fear with Gideon felt like the most natural thing in the world.

The front door opened, and Doc's vet technician ran into the waiting room, pulling her hair up in a ponytail. Waving at Fannie and Gideon as she passed them, she entered the door that led to the back of the facility where the lab was located. She would go into the examination room from there.

"I didn't keep him safe." Fannie sniffed. "Where would he find something like bad meat to make him so sick?" Her voice wobbled on the last few words, and she bit down on her lip to hold back a new onslaught of tears.

"Shh. We don't know for certain what happened." Gideon handed her his clean handkerchief and waited for her to use it before wrapping his arm around her shoulders and pulling her back to his side. "No matter what, it's not your fault."

"All my life I've been taught to accept whatever happens as God's will. That's hard to do sometimes." She looked up at Gideon. "If he was poisoned, I don't *want* to forgive that person." She sighed. "I'm a terrible Amish woman." Fresh tears welled in her eyes.

Gideon squeezed her shoulders. "No. You're human. I believe when an innocent is hurt, righteous anger is justified."

"You've been away from us. Of course you would think that."

Gideon smiled down at her. "Tell you what. You can talk to me about your anger while you work through it and come to whatever conclusion a good Amish woman like you would come to. In the meantime, I won't tattle to the bishop. Okay?"

Heaving a sigh, Fannie nodded. Her conscience didn't feel better, but time to figure out her true feelings would help.

Leland came in carrying cups of coffee and pastries from a local bakery. He took a seat to wait with them.

Too worried to feel hungry, Fannie sipped the hot brew and picked at the cheese Danish. Beside her, Gideon finished his pastry in a few bites. The crisis had not affected his appetite. She handed him the other half of her pastry with a watery smile.

When Doc Silva stepped into the room, Fannie rose. Gideon stood at her side. She grasped his hand needing his strength.

The veterinarian's expression was grim. "We've stabilized him, but he isn't out of the woods."

The breath Fannie had been holding swooshed out. Titus was alive.

"It's as you thought." He looked at Gideon. "He was poisoned."

Gideon stiffened.

"We identified arsenic in the sample you gave me. It's good you brought it. Most people don't remember to bring one, or don't know they should."

Anger flared in Fannie. "Will there be any permanent damage?" Her voice shook.

"I don't believe so. Fortunately, he's a big boy. That worked in his favor. We've begun fluid and drug therapy." He frowned. "Do you know how he got it?"

"No." Fannie shook her head.

Gideon remained silent, but his eyes burned hot.

"I'm going to have to keep him here for a few days. You'll need to look around and find the source so he can't get into it again."

Fannie looked at Gideon and then at the vet. "Titus never leaves his girls."

Gideon squeezed her hand. "Whatever he got into has to be there in the pasture. We'll find it."

Fannie gasped. Fear speared through her. "The goats! We have to go and look *now*."

With hasty goodbyes, they left the vet's office. Gideon helped Fannie into Leland's truck.

She slid to the middle of the seat where she sat wedged between the two men. Consumed with worry for the goats, she forgot to put on the seat belt. Only when Gideon dangled the buckle in front of her face did she remember.

Leland broke the heavy silence. "Where would that dog get into arsenic?"

"Don't know. First thing I can think of that contains arsenic is rat poison." Gideon stared straight ahead.

Fannie clutched her hands together in her lap. "We have barn cats and live traps. Samuel doesn't allow the use of chemicals." Her voice broke.

Gideon's hand covered hers, keeping her from lifting it to her cheek.

She looked up at him. His green eyes held a turbulence she'd never seen in them.

"We'll walk the pasture together."

She nodded and looked down at his large hand covering hers. "Danke." He would help her. For that she was glad.

Thanking Leland for the ride, Gideon walked with Fannie to the barn. She may feel guilty about her anger, but he had no such qualms. If someone had deliberately poisoned Titus, he'd insist she speak to the sheriff.

Of course, anger wasn't all he was dealing with. Frustration boiled in him today too. During this morning's crisis, he'd wished he'd had his truck. Time had been wasted running to Leland's for transport. What if the next medical emergency involved Fannie?

He took a deep breath, reminding himself that his family, and Fannie's family, had lived without automobiles all their lives. He'd chosen to return to this life.

He rubbed his hand down his face. Before making the decision to come back, he'd spent a great deal of time thinking about the inconveniences he'd encounter. What he hadn't considered were life-threatening crises where time mattered.

Gideon opened the milk-room door for Fannie. Lucy stood at the sink.

Fannie rushed inside. "Aunt Lucy. Let me help."

"How is Titus?" Fannie's aunt was washing up the pails and having trouble holding the spray nozzle. She showered the room and everyone in it.

Gideon ducked the arc of water and turned off the faucet.

In the milking parlor, a bucket clattered to the cement floor. He and Fannie followed Lucy into the parlor.

"*Susie*. Dear me," murmured Aunt Lucy.

Fannie brushed past her aunt and stopped short. Gideon looked over her shoulder.

The normally spotless room gave new meaning to the words *milk paint*.

Rich goat milk was splashed across the wall. Milk dripped from the milk stand and puddled on the floor before slowly making its way to the wash drain.

Susie stared at the mess in shock. Her blue skirts were stained dark from the wet milk dripping off her hems and onto the floor.

Tulip stood on the milk stand, bleating and carrying on as if she were the sacrificial goat for an Old Testament offering.

Dodging around the milky puddle, Fannie released the nanny, who jumped down and trotted out the door to join the herd loafing in the barn.

"We thought we would help." Susie's expression crumpled in disappointment.

Lucy peeked through the door, her fingers fiddling with a tie on her Kapp. "We didn't know how long you would be gone."

A problem a telephone could have easily solved. Gideon shoved the thought aside. "Stay there, Lucy." Gideon took Susie's hand and led her past the milk. "Don't slip and fall. One medical emergency for the day is more than enough."

Fannie began to unwind the short garden hose attached to a wall spigot. "Danke for your help. We'll finish up."

Seeing the aunts out, Gideon took the mop from Fannie. "Let me do that. You check on the does."

By the time he'd hosed down the walls and floor, mopped, and checked he'd gotten all the splatter, Fannie had examined her girls and finished processing the milk. Together, they transferred it to the refrigerator in the washhouse.

Gideon wiped his hands on his trousers. "Ready to walk around the pasture?" He would have preferred to do this task on his own but knew she would insist on seeing what had poisoned Titus.

"Yes." She straightened her shoulders. "I kept the herd indoors as a precaution."

Since he'd first lain eyes on the sick dog, Gideon's gut had been knotted with apprehension. He had seen the natural measures Fannie and Samuel took to keep the farm organic. He knew of nothing on the farm that would contain high levels of arsenic. Which left only one other conclusion: Someone had placed arsenic in the pasture.

"We'll walk the perimeter first. If we don't find anything, we'll crisscross the center."

Her answer was to walk to the fence and begin the journey around the edges of the field.

The sun beat down on Gideon's shoulders as he walked at Fannie's side. Cabbage white butterflies fluttered like summer snowflakes over yellow dandelions and clover.

They entered the brush, where sparrows flitted through the leafy tops the goats couldn't reach. Moving slowly, they kept their eyes on the ground looking for anything out of the ordinary, while trying not to get poked by the lower branches that were bare of green growth.

In the section where the fence had been cut, Gideon retraced his steps. So close to the road, this property was easily accessible.

On his fourth pass over the same area, Fannie huffed. "You've already looked there, Gideon. Several times."

He ducked beneath a bush, pushing aside grapevines stripped of their leaves. "I have to admit, I expected to find something here."

"Because this is where the fence was cut?"

The edge in her voice gave him pause. He came out from beneath the bush and straightened up. "Yes." He walked up to the wire. The grass on the other side stood tall all the way into the gully and up again by the road. Had someone walked through it, there would have been a noticeable trail.

"You still think the cut wire was something more than a prank?" She stood beside him and, for the first time, seemed to be entertaining the idea that whoever had cut her fence had not done so in innocent fun.

"You know I do."

"At least you're honest and consistent."

She made that sound like a bad thing, which might have tickled his funny bone if the situation wasn't so serious. "C'mon. Let's see if there's anything in the bog."

Breaking away from the brush, they were careful not to get caught in the muddy bottom pasture. Gideon took the lead, helping Fannie step from one clump of wiry grass to the next. The occasional *ribbits* of green frogs accompanied them.

Halfway across the wetland, Gideon turned to help Fannie step off one tussock and onto another. He held out his hand. Without hesitation, she placed her hand in his and took the step. The toe of her shoe touched the grass and slid off landing with a splash in the muck.

Her shriek rang in Gideon's ear. He grabbed her other hand and pulled her up. Circling his arm around her, he hauled her onto solid ground. For one breathless moment, they stood close.

The gold flecks in Fannie's wide eyes shimmered brightly before she pulled away.

His heart raced. He didn't want to let her go. They needed to talk about what he'd said to her beneath the tent at the barn raising. But today was too soon. Until he was well on his way to being baptized, she would not want to talk about the future.

She looked down in disgust at her filthy shoe. Leaning her weight on that foot produced a squishing sound. "I'm going to smell like the bottom of the bog."

He contemplated her shoe. "Does that smell better or worse than what's found on the floor of the barn?"

Her half-hearted chuckle lifted his mood a fraction. They would get through this crisis okay. "Good. I'm glad to hear you laugh."

Her smile faded, and he wished he could take the words back.

"Titus could have died. He's not out of danger yet." As fast as she'd laughed, a tear welled up and glistened in her eye.

"C'mon." Gideon brushed past her, afraid that if they lingered he'd do something stupid like pull her back into his arms.

He led her out of the swamp and into the thick brush that thrived along the damp edges. They were at the greatest possible distance from the house. This corner of the pasture backed up to a copse of trees separating it from Leland's cornfield.

Gideon lifted a branch up for Fannie to pass beneath without catching her Kapp or hair on the twigs. Crouching low, he followed her. He spied something white near the base of a willow bush.

"Wait up, Fannie."

She turned back. "Did you find something?"

On his hands and knees, Gideon crawled to the trunk of the bush and found an open margarine container. He stretched to look inside and took a sniff. The brick-colored smears on the interior made his skin crawl. "I think I have it."

Falling to her knees, Fannie crawled beneath the bush with him. "What do you think was in there?"

He reached up and tore green leaves from the bush. They would have to do as a barrier between his fingers and the container. "Based on the smell, my guess is this container held ground beef laced with arsenic."

The color drained from Fannie's face. She stared at the container. "Someone baited Titus?"

Honest and consistent. How he wished he didn't have to be in this case. "I would say that's right." Gideon crawled from beneath the willow.

She scrambled after him. "They knew he would eat the meat and get sick? Maybe die?"

He didn't answer her. She'd come to the correct conclusion on her own.

"Are you sure that's what we're looking for?" She glanced about like she couldn't believe their search had come to an end.

"We can always come back and search some more if this isn't what I think it is."

Her eyes narrowed. "Why are you holding the container with leaves?"

"I don't want my fingerprints on it." To avoid going back through the bog, he walked in the direction that would take them across the open field.

Fannie followed, her limp noticeable. "To get fingerprints would involve calling the sheriff."

Hallelujah. The woman had caught on. "That's right."

"I'm not sure we should do that."

Gideon stopped short, blocking her way. "Titus almost died. You don't believe a crime has been committed?"

Breathing hard to catch her breath, she stared at the container he held. Uncertainty flashed across her face.

Gideon took the opportunity to press his point. "This," he said, holding up the container, "was not a mischievous prank. This was a calculated attempt to kill your dog."

Her bow lips flattened into a thin line. "You believe the cut fence and this are related?" She shook her head. "What reason would someone have to do these things, Gideon?"

"I don't know." He fought to hold onto his patience, reminding himself not to let his anger at an unknown vandal spill over onto the sweet woman standing in front of him. "You said earlier I was honest and consistent. I believe they are connected and not random acts. Someone has a purpose behind them. And we need to find that person so we can learn why they are doing these things."

Her face contorted, and her hand covered her mouth.

Feeling like he'd kicked a puppy, Gideon wrapped his free arm around her shoulders and nudged her forward. "This is bigger than us,

Fannie. At least I think it is. We need help from the sheriff, if for no other reason than we have to be sure something worse doesn't happen."

"Like what?"

He could think of a million and one things. "I don't know." There went his honesty, but he didn't want to answer her knee-jerk question. The atrocities running through his mind had been put there over years of watching crime shows on television. Better to let her come up with her own, less horrific answers. "I want to go to Leland's and call the sheriff."

Beneath his arm, her shoulders slumped. He'd won the argument.

When they arrived at the house, Gideon placed the container in a brown paper bag and handed it to Fannie. "Promise you won't let anyone touch it."

"I promise." She held the bag away from her as if she were afraid it would bite.

Leaving her to explain the significance of the container to her aunts, Gideon raced to the freezer shed on Leland's property. Using Fannie's key, he entered the shed and went directly to the desk. He ran his finger down the handwritten list of numbers. The sheriff's number wasn't there. *No surprise.* Instead of involving law enforcement, the Amish chose to forgive. It was their way.

He paused in punching in the number for Information.

It's our way.

He'd come home to take his place among them. They were his people. He was counting on their predisposition to forgive. The Kings had forgiven him. He hoped his family would do the same someday.

Getting through to the operator, Gideon picked a pencil from the can on the desk and added the number for the sheriff's office to the list. Forgiving someone was fine and dandy. But in order to do that, he first wanted to know who he needed to forgive. He hoped the sheriff could help him with that.

13

Fannie grunted as she heaved a tote of supplies into the back of the market wagon.

Gideon came out of the house and down the steps carrying another one. "Your aunts are nearly ready to go."

Fannie looked longingly toward the pasture. "Am I doing the right thing?" She'd made the difficult decision to leave the herd without a guardian. The flea market's Saturday crowd would be too much for her aunts to handle on their own. By midday, they would be tired and ready to go shopping or meet a friend for tea.

Gideon stowed the tote and walked over to stand at her side. "Do you want me to stay here, Fannie?"

She knew how much he'd been looking forward to going to the flea market today. "I've asked Leland and Samuel to come by and check on the girls. And, truthfully, I may need your help at the booth. I don't believe my aunts have the stamina for a full day. The crowds will be heavy."

Gideon slipped his arm around her shoulder.

Astonished, she drew in a breath and put her hand on her cheek, which was growing warm with a blush.

He pulled her hand away from her face. Beneath the brim of his hat, his eyes studied her. "You can't be in two places at once. Rest in the knowledge you've done the best you can under the circumstances and leave everything else to God."

She dared to lean into his side, liking the weight of his arm across her shoulders. "It's hard not to worry."

"Do you need to give Daffodil another talking-to before we go?" He raised an eyebrow.

Fannie snickered. "No. I've already spoken to her twice about her responsibilities."

"Then let's go in and move your aunts along."

They walked to the house hand in hand. The feel of his rough palm against her softer skin sent delicious shivers through her.

The heights of her happiness and depths of her sadness were giving her emotional vertigo. Every day that passed, her heart belonged more and more to Gideon, filling her with a joy she'd never before known. The heartache in the midst of the joy was that he hadn't yet been baptized into the church. He had obstacles to overcome before that could happen.

Then there was Titus. Her beautiful herd guardian. How would she have ever handled the last few days without Gideon by her side?

The sheriff had taken the margarine container and had it tested. The results had come back positive for arsenic.

Goosebumps prickled up Fannie's arms at the memory.

Gideon had never answered her question about what other things might happen if this was more than a malicious prank. The sheriff, however, had no qualms telling her. If he hoped to scare her into cooperating with him, the tactic worked. She'd barely slept a wink the last three nights.

Titus was still in the animal hospital receiving therapy for the poison he'd ingested. She missed him, and she could tell the nannies missed him too.

Gideon opened the kitchen door for her.

There was a flurry of movement in front of the window.

Aunt Susie and Aunt Lucy stood side by side next to the table, eyes wide with innocence.

"You were watching us, weren't you?" The assertion was a statement of fact that held no malice. Fannie started to pull her hand from Gideon's, but he held on.

She looked at him and basked in the tenderness of his smile.

The aunts sighed in unison.

"Ach." Flustered, Fannie snatched her hand from Gideon's. "We have to get moving or we'll be late." Fannie had never flounced in her life. With her limp, flouncing wasn't something she did. But if she could have managed it, she would have. Instead, she had to be satisfied with a quick exit into the office to grab her tote bag.

Fannie placed the last of the inventory on the tables covered in green cloths. As members of a small business co-op, they took a turn manning the booth at the flea market. Today was her aunts' turn.

"I got you *Kaffie* and apple fritters." Gideon stepped into the booth and set his purchases down.

"Danke, Gideon." She liked that he'd begun sprinkling Pennsylvania Dutch in among his English words.

"Ooooh." Aunt Lucy opened the paper bag of fritters and lifted one out. "Danke."

Fannie giggled over her aunt's enthusiasm for the treat, which was the size of a dinner plate.

His eyes twinkled. As the first tourist bus roared into the parking lot, he raised his foam cup in a salute to her. "Figured you could use the energy."

Fannie smiled. "You figured right." Sitting on one of the folding chairs behind the register, she tore the sticky pastry in half and passed him a piece before taking a bite. This could be her last chance to sit down for the next several hours.

Accepting the sweet, Gideon wandered around the tables looking at the variety of handcrafted items on display. "How much do you usually sell?"

"On a sunny summer day like today, we'll sell nearly all of it."

Keeping a permanent booth at the entrance to one of the large buildings and selling a variety of merchandise—from fresh meat to expensive furniture—the co-op had a premium spot in the market.

Two women dressed in cotton T-shirts and denim jeans came around the corner of the building. They wore floppy sun hats and sunglasses, and carried large tote bags. They were prepared to shop.

Gideon leaned close to Fannie's ear and whispered, "Showtime."

Poking him, she whispered back, "Don't you know showtime and humility don't mix?"

He snorted and took the empty foam cup from her hand. His fingertips felt cool as they brushed across her knuckles. "Just saying. You'll sell more if you say a few 'Ah-mish' words."

Cracking up over his silly accent, Fannie wiped the last of the apple fritter crumbs from her hands and stood to welcome her customers. From the first day she began helping her aunts, she'd treated each customer like a guest. And when they left the booth she always said, "Danke."

Gideon stepped out of the booth and watched Fannie as she worked with the customers crowding around the tables. Whether a local woman came through doing her weekly shopping, or a bevy of tourists rolled through looking for bargains and sneaking pictures,

Fannie was pleasant and happy to serve them. He would have to work on his patience if he was to help her. He'd never had an abundance of that particular virtue.

In a matter of minutes the booth became so crowded he could only see the top of Fannie's Kapp, so he left to explore the market and see for himself if it was as diverse as he remembered.

He made his way along the edges of the buildings to avoid the thickest of the crowd. Following the signs, he found the sales floor for small animals and fowl. Gawking tourists mingled with the serious buyers. He'd forgotten how noisy this sales floor got with all the crowing, quacking, and honking.

Across the room, Doc Silva inspected incoming animals for health problems before allowing them on the sales floor. Hoping for an update on Titus, Gideon worked his way through the crowd to the vet.

Having performed this service every Saturday morning for years, Doc Silva knew what he was looking for and quickly waved the healthy animals through.

When the line dwindled to last-minute stragglers, Gideon stepped forward. Not wanting to waste the vet's time, he got right to the point. "How's Titus doing this morning?"

The vet smiled. "He's doing well."

Gideon exhaled. "Fannie will be happy to hear that."

The vet's brow crinkled. "That dog has amazed me. When I first saw him, I wasn't sure he'd live through that first day. Didn't want to say anything to Fannie until I knew for sure."

Gideon nodded, not wanting to think of Fannie's reaction if Titus had died.

The vet motioned to a man carrying an animal crate. "He'll be able to come home in another day or two. I want to be sure all of the poison is out of his system."

"Danke." Gideon left the vet checking a batch of lop-eared bunnies.

Merging into the moving crowd of browsers, Gideon passed a booth selling hand-knitted socks jammed cheek to jowl with a booth selling strawberries and sweet corn. On one side of the aisle, they were serving up Mexican tacos; on the other side, Amish whoopie pies. The diversity of food choices made his decision for lunch difficult.

Walking past a booth selling used garden and farming tools, Gideon stopped to look at an antique cultivator when he heard a familiar voice.

Abram stood inside the booth talking to the merchant.

Gideon's first impulse was to barge in and face his brother. Born and raised Amish, he knew he should be less confrontational. Somehow, he'd missed getting that gene when it was handed out. Unless he'd had it at one time and, after years living like the English, the gene had been buried deep beneath a few other character flaws, like impatience. Because right this minute, he wanted to grab his brother and shake him till his teeth rattled, then hug him so hard his wide-brimmed felt hat popped off his head.

With steely determination, Gideon walked away. Would he ever have the opportunity to speak to Abram? Up one aisle and down the next, blind to the people and the wares for sale, Gideon tried to walk off his discontent, but he only grew more exasperated with the situation.

Passing a booth that sold extra-large cups of coffee, he stopped to purchase a cup. In a moment of inspiration, he purchased two. He'd face Abram with a peace offering. Would that help his cause? It couldn't hurt. And something in both hands might remind Gideon to keep his frustration in check.

Carrying the coffees, Gideon went looking for Abram.

His brother had stepped out of the tool booth and was talking to another man in the aisle, in front of a crowded little cubbyhole that sold pet supplies.

Sitting on a nearby bench, Gideon waited for Abram to move on.

With the ebb and flow of the crowd, Gideon followed him into the part of the flea market that held overflow booths during the busy season. Open to the air, the sun beat down unmercifully on the tables set up on either side of the wide aisle.

The coffee Gideon carried was growing cold, and he was beginning to think this wasn't the best idea he'd ever had. Feeling like a creepy stalker, he needed to make his move before he talked himself out of his plan. He wanted to talk to Abram in this section where there were fewer people to witness whatever happened. Unfortunately, that was the full extent of his strategy. It wasn't groundbreaking, but it was the only plan he had.

At the end of the aisle, where the flea market ended and rows and rows of visitor's cars and trucks began, Gideon approached his brother.

"Abram."

His brother whirled around. Face shaded by his hat brim, Abram stared hard at Gideon before turning away.

"Wait." Gideon stepped up beside him, prepared to walk at his side until he got answers to his questions. "Why won't you speak to me?"

Silent, Abram kept walking.

"I've come to rebuild my life, Abram. The life I left. My family is a big part of that."

Abram stopped his headlong rush to wherever he wanted to be, which was not with Gideon. Standing tall, he shook his head. "I will not fellowship with a man who steals from his parents. They did nothing but love and nurture you through childhood. And that's how you repay them?"

Shock froze Gideon in place. Of all the things he'd expected his brother to say, this was so far out there, he didn't know where to begin asking questions. "Huh?"

Abram shook his head in disgust and started walking.

Gideon hurried after him. "What are you talking about? I never took anything from Mamm and Daed. I'm not a thief."

Fire brimmed in Abram's eyes, breaking through the aloof exterior he'd tried to maintain. "That first Christmas you were gone. How I hated you. A sin, yes, but I couldn't stop hating you."

The venom in his brother's voice cut Gideon to his core.

"It appears you haven't ceased hating me. What happened that Christmas?" Gideon's voice cracked.

"There was little that year in the way of gifts or treats. Mamm did the best she could, but I was a kid and disappointed."

Their parents never talked about money in front the children, but Gideon knew they weren't poor. They'd always had money for gifts and extras. "I don't understand. Why?"

"Daed said, 'Gideon took the money.'"

"What?"

"That's what Daed said to Mamm late one night. I overheard them talking. 'Gideon took the money.'" For the first time, instead of walking the other way, Abram stepped closer to Gideon. "Why? That's all I want to know. Why would you steal from your parents before leaving?"

"I didn't. I swear. I didn't take any money."

Abram frowned. "Swearing is forbidden. There seem to be things you've forgotten."

Hadn't Fannie said the same thing to him?

Gideon shook his head and thought back twelve years to the day he'd left. "I don't know what you heard, or thought you heard, but I did not steal from Mamm and Daed. I sold my buggy and used that as well as money saved from other jobs when I left." Gideon sank to a nearby bench.

Abram stood over him, unrelenting in his anger.

Setting the cups of coffee on the ground at his feet, Gideon rubbed his hands down his face. Elbows on his knees, he tried to think through what Abram had said. "I didn't take anything from them. I don't suppose you'll believe me."

Reluctantly, Abram sat ramrod straight beside him. "It wasn't only about the money." His throat worked like he had something stuck in it. "The day you left, you took all the happiness in our home with you. Mamm and Daed were never the same after that."

The ache in Gideon's heart increased tenfold. When Abram stood to leave, Gideon didn't try to stop him. His brother walked away, leaving Gideon with two cups of cold coffee and a monumental burden in his heart.

14

Fannie settled on the wagon seat and sighed with relief. Her hip and leg were on fire, and her feet ached fiercely.

Gideon pointed Fiona toward home. From the back seat of the wagon came the sound of snoring. Aunt Susie and Aunt Lucy were already napping after the hectic day they'd had. Fannie wasn't sure how they had kept going, but the fast pace had finally caught up with them at the end of the very profitable day.

Along with the regular tour buses, additional buses had arrived with folks ready to purchase souvenirs to take home. One woman had been especially enthusiastic about Aunt Susie and Aunt Lucy's soap. She had filled a shopping bag to give as gifts.

"Danke for talking to Doc Silva about Titus."

Gideon's smile was wan, but at least it was there.

She brushed imaginary dust from her skirts. "I'll be so glad when he finally comes home. I miss him terribly. The nannies do too. They're used to having him in the field with them."

"I know." He reached over and took her hand in his.

Her heart gave a soft bump. For all the good news, there was one little fly in Fannie's happiness ointment. Gideon had come back from his excursion through the market minus his good mood and happy smile.

For lunch, he'd brought turkey club sandwiches back to the booth. He'd been pale. Not the laughing jokester who had teased her about pouring on the Amish authenticity to make sales. He'd been solemn the entire time he helped her work the booth and close it up.

She missed the silly man she'd shared an apple fritter with a few hours before. Her imagination ran wild, and the worry was making her sick. "Did you enjoy today?"

He was quiet for so long she thought he wasn't going to answer. "I talked to Abram."

Fannie's heart leaped with delight before remembering he wasn't the least bit happy. Something must have gone terribly wrong. "It didn't go well?"

"It didn't."

Despite itching to know what had transpired between the two brothers, Fannie held her tongue. Gideon's trouble with his brother was none of her business. Except this was Gideon, and what happened to him was important to her. More so with each day that passed, which gave her the courage to ask, "What did he say?"

"He hates me."

"He said that?"

"Jah. In those words."

"Why? Surely his reason isn't worthy of hanging on to so much anger after all these years."

"He thinks I stole money from my parents." Tension radiated from him.

"Why would he think such a thing?" Really, the man needed to spill the entire conversation instead of giving it to her piecemeal.

"The first year after I left home, Christmas was lean. Abram was a kid and disappointed. At some point, he said he overheard my Mamm and Daed say that I'd stolen money from them."

Shock waves reverberated through Fannie. She could only stare at him. Any questions she had flew out of her head into the late afternoon air.

"I didn't steal from them. I would never do that." He looked at her, his eyes snapping with indignation.

"I believe you." And she did, with absolute certainty.

"I don't know what he heard, but I'm not a thief."

"You have to talk to your parents, Gideon. When they get home from visiting Joshua, you must go see them and ask them what Abram could have heard." *And that brother of yours needs to go to the bishop and confess his unforgiving attitude.* She thought it best to keep that thought to herself.

"I will. I didn't steal any money. But something did happen for them to have a lean Christmas that year. Twelve years have passed. I hope they're able to remember." A quiet determination wove its way through his words.

He was quiet the rest of the ride home. Fannie didn't have the heart to try and distract him. He was upset, and rightfully so.

When they turned into the lane leading home, Fannie was relieved. She was exhausted, and they still had the wagon to unload and the goats to care for. Thankfully, the kids nursed through the day so she wasn't milking in the evenings.

In the back seat, Aunt Susie roused from her nap. "Lucy, wake up. We're home."

Aunt Lucy snorted and sat up. "We're here?"

"Yes, sister. Get a move on."

Approaching the house, Fannie scanned the pasture, bewildered because she didn't see any of the goats. "Where are they?"

Gideon reined in Fiona and set the brake. Jumping off the wagon, he helped her down and then helped her aunts.

Fannie called out. Limping to the gate, she listened for the bells, but heard nothing. She called again, but there were no answering bleats.

Gideon stepped up beside her. "Maybe they're in the bottom of the pasture."

Fear burned in Fannie's chest as she opened the gate.

Gideon followed her, latching the gate behind them. He took her hand. "We'll look together." He had a glint of determination in his eyes.

Thankful for his presence and his strength, she set off with him, following the fence along the perimeter.

Gideon matched his pace to Fannie's slower gait. She wanted to tell him not to wait for her, but to go and find the goats. At the same time, she didn't want him to leave her side or let go of her hand. The feeling of panic rising inside her was becoming all too familiar.

They dipped and wove through the brush. Fannie called out and listened for the telltale jingle of the bells and the distinct bleats of each of her nannies. But every call was met with silence.

Reaching the portion of the fence that ran along the side of the road, Gideon insisted on staying close to the wire. He pulled up short and squeezed Fannie's hand to bring her to a halt. "Watch where you step."

She looked past him. Her heart dropped with a sickening thud. The wire fence had been cut and pulled back. Horror rocketed through her. The grass around the hole in the fence lay flat. Clods of soil were churned into the grass where many hooves had passed through.

The trembling started in Fannie's legs and rippled upward taking over her entire body until she shook uncontrollably.

Gideon wrapped his arms around her holding her close. "We'll find them, Fannie. Don't give up hope."

Tears of anguish welled in her eyes and spilled in a hot flood. Her choking sobs built to wails of grief. "This is all my fault. What have I done?"

Gideon had thought the day couldn't get any worse. He'd been wrong.

"Oh, Fannie." He pulled her close. "Don't blame yourself."

Her cheek rested on his chest and tears spilled from her eyes. Her gut-wrenching sobs tore at his heart. She shook so hard he was afraid she'd fall apart. He tightened his grip on her as if trying to hold her together.

Her words were punctuated with tiny gasps and hiccups. "I shouldn't have left them today."

Holding her close, Gideon shuddered to think what might have happened to her if she'd been on the farm alone and tried to stop whoever had done this. "Shh. You don't know if your presence at the house would have prevented this."

"They're all gone. Not even a kid left behind."

That was the part that surprised him. The herd wasn't large, but there were too many goats to fit into the back of a pickup truck. Something larger had been used. He looked over the top of her Kapp. The grass was trampled beyond the fence all the way to the road. "I'll call the sheriff."

"I'm going with you." She wiped her eyes and looked at him defiantly as if she expected an argument from him.

"Let's go then."

When she stepped away, Gideon felt bereft. He led her back the way they had come, holding her small hand in his. The walk would have been easier if he'd released her hand, but he didn't want to do that. The way she clung to him gave him hope that she felt the same way.

The Grossdawdi Haus was in sight when the door opened and Micah raced down the steps followed by Fannie's aunts.

"Where are the goats, Tante Fannie?" He jumped and skipped around her, eager for news.

Her voice held traces of tears. "We can't find any of them. The fence was cut again. We're going to Leland's to call the sheriff."

"I'll tell Mamm and Daed." Filled with important news, he dashed off at a dead run.

"What can we do?" Susie stood on the top step, worry lines etched deep in her brow. Lucy stood behind her in the doorway.

He didn't want to frighten them, but Gideon had to be honest with them. "We don't know who did this or why. Stay indoors. We'll be back right after we speak to the sheriff."

Fiona stood patiently between the shafts of the wagon. Fannie was already perched on the seat. Gideon jumped on beside her and turned the horse in the direction of Leland's property.

Fannie sniffed and rubbed her eyes. "I should have stayed home today."

"No. I should have stayed here." Not for a minute would he allow Fannie to blame herself for what happened.

"You?" Her look was skeptical, as if he'd claimed he had three extra toes on one foot.

"You have driven your aunts to the market many Saturdays before I came on the scene. You could have driven them this morning." *And I could have avoided the ugly scene with my brother.* Except, if he'd done that, he still wouldn't know Abram's reason for wanting nothing to do with him.

Fannie didn't reply. She studied the field of corn, Fiona's harness, and her hands. She looked anywhere but at him, which was puzzling, but he was tired enough that he might be reading her all wrong.

Arriving in Leland's yard, he reined Fiona in at the shed.

Not waiting for Gideon to help her, Fannie stepped down from the wagon. "I'm glad you came with us."

The words were murmured so softly Gideon almost didn't hear them.

He willed her to look at him so he could see her expression and be certain he'd heard her correctly. But she was unlocking the door of the shed.

Swinging off the seat, he followed her inside.

Hands on her hips, she stood in front of the phone. "I'm making the call."

"Okay." Liking this feisty side of Fannie, he pointed out the number he'd added to the list. Was it only a few days ago he'd done that? He crossed his arms and leaned back against the wall so she could make the call without him hovering. She answered the sheriff's questions with confidence, which made him feel more than a little proud of her. He'd never tell her, though. She'd accuse him of sinning.

Did she realize the shell she'd wrapped herself in for years had begun to crumble? Each day she shed bigger and bigger chunks of her old self. The beautiful woman emerging was someone he wanted by his side for a lifetime.

Gideon dropped his hands to his side. His thoughts bounced back to the day of the barn raising. Yes, that afternoon had certainly done the trick. A lifetime with Fannie. He'd fallen in love with a woman who wasn't fully convinced he'd be around next month, never mind a lifetime.

He'd just have to convince her. And himself.

Fannie hung up the phone and took a deep, fortifying breath. "That's done. He's coming out to take a look."

Gideon pushed away from the wall and resettled his hat. "Ready to head back to the house?"

She brushed past him, fire in her eyes. "We should tell Leland. He can make calls and spread the word so others will keep a close watch on their herds and flocks."

Gideon followed her out of the building. "Maybe someone will see your herd." She stopped short, and he bumped into her. He grabbed her arms to keep her upright. "Don't do that."

"What?" Puzzled, her brows drew together.

"Stop so fast I run into you."

A quick frown was her only acknowledgment of his admonishment before she took off again, skirt swishing with each step. "If someone sees them, they should call the sheriff." She walked up the front steps of Leland's home and knocked on his door. "The more people looking for my goats, the greater chance I have of getting them back."

Gideon followed her, hoping and praying that would be the case.

15

The following day was church Sunday. Fannie awoke clinging to the faint hope the goats had been returned in the night. The sheriff hadn't encouraged the notion, but his job surely gave him a dark view of the world. She'd gone to bed hoping the dawn of a new day would bring answers to her prayers.

Still amazed she'd found the courage to make the call to the sheriff, Fannie dressed in her barn clothes. Fear for her nannies and kids, and yes, a bit of anger, had given her the courage to take that bold step.

Leaving the quiet house, she walked to the empty barn, straining to hear the softest bleat, the gentlest tinkle of a bell. But the only sound was the birds singing their morning chorus high in the maple tree. Fannie covered a jaw-splitting yawn. Worry had kept her awake through the night.

She was adding fresh water to the trough when Gideon stepped into the barn.

Seeing the fresh hay in the wall manger, he quirked an eyebrow at her. "What's this? One phone call to the sheriff and now you do unnecessary chores on Sunday too?" He shook his head in mock horror.

Fannie narrowed her eyes and wiggled the business end of the hose in his direction. Preparing for the goats' homecoming kept her hope alive. "I'm praying they'll come home today." Turning off the spigot, she coiled the hose on the rack while Gideon helped smooth out the kinks. "I keep going over and over in my mind what I could have done differently yesterday."

"Dwelling on how things could have happened will drive you crazy, Fannie."

She entered the milk room and grabbed the broom to sweep the already clean floor. "I know it's silly." Her voice wobbled, and she swept faster. "But I have this fear that if I stop thinking about them, they'll be gone forever."

Gideon walked up behind her and placed his hand on the broom handle, stopping her frantic sweeping. "You can't protect them from afar, Fannie. Only God can do that."

Her shoulders shook.

Gideon spun her around letting the broom drop to the floor.

She gave up the fight not to weep and let him gather her into his arms.

He rested his cheek on the top of her head. "Ah, Fannie. Your tears rip my heart to shreds."

Leaning into him, she let the warmth of his arms melt the chilly block of fear in her chest. His touch had become familiar to her. "I'm doing the chores because I need to stay busy."

"Jah. Trust me, I know." He ran his hand down her arm. "After Jacob's death, I tried to work myself into the grave."

She tipped her head back to look at him. "That wouldn't bring him back."

His green eyes were dark with memories. "No, but I felt I needed to do penance for what happened." He hesitated, closed his eyes for a moment, then opened them. "His death was an accident. But it was by my hand he lost his life."

Fannie gasped. She lifted her hand to his jaw. "I'm sorry."

He wanted to stop right there. Let her touch distract him from telling her the rest. But he didn't. He'd begun. He would finish. "Benjamin, the boy at the barn raising—he's Jacob's brother."

What Gideon was telling her was so unbelievable, Fannie wanted to make him stop talking and help her sort out what he was saying, but she didn't. He needed to share the weight of what had happened with someone. He'd chosen her.

"That was the first time I'd spoken to Jacob's parents about what happened." He cleared his throat. "For the longest time, I hated that he died and not me."

Gripping his arms, she pushed away from him in shock. "That would not bring him back."

"And you worrying until you make yourself ill will not bring back the goats."

She sighed, deflated by the pinprick of his logic. "That's true, Gideon. But they are *goats*. You can't compare them to your friend Jacob. And I still have the hope of seeing my does again. You don't have that same hope." She looked into his eyes praying she hadn't overstepped the bounds of their relationship.

His green gaze remained clear and direct.

"You can't question God's ways, Gideon."

"That's what Jacob's father said."

She whispered, "When God calls a person home, another cannot take their place." She cupped his face in her hand. "You are meant to be here."

Heat flared in his gaze. He pulled her close again. "And I thank God every day that I am here."

Wrapped in his arms, Fannie's heart trembled. *So do I.* Beneath her cheek, his chest expanded and then relaxed in a sigh.

With the tip of his finger beneath her chin, he tipped her face up. "C'mon. I smell bacon frying."

Her hand in his, Fannie walked beside him back to the house. If his objective had been to take her mind off her lost goats, he'd succeeded. Holding her and telling her more about Jacob's death gave her something different to think about, but also another worry to add to her list. Would she survive the heartbreak if he decided he couldn't remain in the community?

Her aunts had prepared her favorite breakfast of French toast with a hint of cinnamon, crisp bacon, and scrambled eggs. Because she loved them and knew they'd made this breakfast hoping to cheer her, Fannie forced down three slices. But even warm French toast drowning in maple syrup didn't lift her spirits.

Throughout the meal, Gideon watched her, but remained silent while her aunts' chatter about the coming day swirled around them.

Excusing herself from the table, Fannie went to her room and dressed in her church dress, cape, and apron. Rachel and John Stoltzfus were hosting church this week. Her friend would be in a tizzy about now. Fortunately, Rachel had three sisters living close by to help on this important day.

Gideon had Fiona hitched by the time Fannie and her aunts were ready to leave the house. After helping her aunts into the buggy, Gideon took Fannie's basket containing cup cheese and jellies, and set it in the footwell. He turned to her. "Are you all right?" Lines bracketed his mouth.

Fannie sighed. "My imagination is working overtime." Though she wanted to stay home in case the goats returned, she climbed into the buggy.

He settled in beside her. He clicked his tongue and Fiona set off down the lane. The ride to the Stoltzfus's took only ten minutes.

Absorbed in her thoughts, Fannie was surprised how fast the time went. Soon the buggies of other church members, all headed for the Stoltzfus Haus, joined them.

Upon their arrival, Rachel pulled Fannie into a warm hug. "I heard about Titus and your goats. You must be beside yourself with worry."

Fannie bit her lip and nodded.

"Well now, let's not get ahead of ourselves." Rachel took Fannie's basket from Gideon and waved him on. "Everyone is watching for them. It's the talk of the kitchen. I'm sure the men in the barn are aware as well. Something will turn up. You wait and see."

"I hope whatever happens will happen soon."

Rachel linked her arm in Fannie's. "I heard Titus got sick?"

It was a leading question in search of information to confirm what was surely being talked about in the kitchen.

"He was poisoned."

Shaking her head, Rachel led Fannie into the house. "I'd heard that but hoped the information was wrong. Who would do that?"

"My question exactly. Gideon and the sheriff think whoever poisoned Titus also took the goats."

The women took their seats for the service. Filing into the sitting room with the others, Fannie settled on the bench among her friends and family. Holding the Ausbund in hand, she hoped she would find comfort in singing the familiar songs.

The men entered, and Fannie spotted Abram among them. He wore his usual stern expression.

Gideon walked into the room before the younger unmarried men. His gaze immediately searched out hers, but there was no jubilation in his eyes to indicate his brother's heart had softened.

The sadness of the situation pressed down on Fannie, magnified by the woes already held in her heart. She blinked back tears, but one escaped. She wiped it away, her hand lingering over her scar. Exhausted, she hid her face in her hands when the preaching started. She hoped she wouldn't make a spectacle of herself if she dozed off.

When the service was over, Fannie entered the kitchen to help with the fellowship meal. Sarah was busy cutting pies and cakes when she spotted Fannie. Laying aside the knife, she murmured something to Bonnie Esh, who stepped in to finish the job.

Sarah put her hand on Fannie's shoulder and whispered, "I'm so sorry. Micah said you called the sheriff?"

Fannie nodded, not completely comfortable with the idea she'd notified the authorities. "This is a huge loss. We're hoping they'll be found."

Sarah wrapped an arm around Fannie and squeezed her tight. "I hope so too."

So often on the receiving end of Sarah's churlish attitude, Fannie wasn't sure what to make of her cousin's sincere display of affection. "Danke."

"You're welcome." Sarah picked up a tray holding plates with slices of strawberry pie. "These are ready to go."

Accepting the tray, Fannie took it into the other room where Bishop Esh and the ordained ministers were seated to begin the fellowship meal.

The afternoon drew to a close, and families packed up to go home. Fannie made sure her aunts were comfortable in the buggy's back seat, then climbed into the front. Gideon followed her.

"I have something to tell you, Gideon."

He winked at Fannie as he answered. "What's that, Aunt Lucy?"

"Bonnie Esh said your parents are coming home *today*." She delivered the information in a breathless rush. "Isn't that *gut* news?"

Fannie sucked in her breath, wondering if Gideon thought her aunt's news was indeed good.

"Yes, it is. Danke for telling me, Aunt Lucy."

He didn't sound ecstatic, but relief flooded through Fannie. She hoped he could find out the truth behind Abram's accusations.

Gideon reined in Fiona at the end of the lane leading to the home where he'd grown up. When Lucy made her announcement yesterday, Fannie had insisted there was no reason to delay his visit. Today he hoped to get answers about Abram's accusation—and maybe start restoring all he had destroyed when he left twelve years ago.

Getting Fiona moving again, he let the memories wash over him as he passed between fields of sweet corn and potatoes.

The house, with its stairstep add-ons, was newly painted. In the bright sunlight, it nearly glowed against the green of the distant pastures where Abram's herd of dairy cows grazed.

The kitchen garden had grown. Cucumbers raced exuberant zucchini squash, their vines inching out of the garden and onto the grassy lawn. Tomato plants, staked and secured, were heavy with green fruit beginning to show the first blush of pink. The feathery tops of carrots nestled in close companionship with the aromatic, fleshy leaves of onions.

"Whoa." Gideon brought Fiona to a halt at the hitching rail beneath the enormous maple tree he'd climbed so many times when he was young. Looking up through the thick leaves, he found the two branches growing side by side. They created the perfect seat for a young boy. Many a Sunday afternoon he'd sat with his back against the tree trunk and his legs stretched along the branches, reading a library book.

Always curious, he'd chosen nonfiction books that told about places he dreamed of visiting. Perhaps the reading had been his downfall. When he made the decision to leave the community, he'd immediately driven to New York City and walked Fifth Avenue. Since that time, he'd hiked in the Rocky Mountains, swum in the Atlantic Ocean, and stood on the shore of the Mississippi River. Life was funny. He'd come full circle and discovered there was no place he'd rather be than home.

Taking a fortifying breath, he walked up the steps of the Grossdawdi Haus and knocked. He wiped his hands on his trousers, hoping he hadn't arrived too early in the morning. Or was it too late? How much did Daed help with the day-to-day operations? Was his arm still in a cast? Did Mamm help with the grandchildren? He turned and looked toward the building where the chuffing of compressed air mingled with the whir of a motor.

The doorknob rattled, and his breath caught in his chest.

The inside door opened.

The screen door softened the lines of his Mamm's face. A puzzled frown creased her brow before recognition unfurled on her face. She gasped and her hand went to her breast.

Not sure if he'd done the right thing showing up out of the blue, he smiled. "Hi, Mamm."

Tears followed her outburst of joy.

A loud thump came from another room. The tread of heavy boots grew closer. His Daed peered over his Mamm's shoulder. Uncertainty was etched in the deep lines of his face as she opened the screen door and spread her arms in welcome.

Gideon didn't hesitate to step across the threshold and into her lavender-scented embrace. The smell of her handmade sachets carried him into the past where hugs from Mamm were an everyday occurrence.

He scrunched his eyes and choked back tears.

Her embrace was familiar yet different. Her arms were less muscular, and she was shorter than he remembered. Or was he taller? Age and a lifetime of hard work had taken its toll on her body.

Though ecstatic that she hadn't slammed the door in his face, he came up for air with a hint of trepidation. Gideon wasn't sure if his Daed would welcome him with the same enthusiasm.

Leaning away from his mother, Gideon met his father's gaze.

The moist tears running down the weathered face and into the silver beard were all he needed to send him into the warm circle of his father's arms.

"Welcome home, son."

"Daed. It's good to be home." The words came out in a broken murmur. The arms around him tightened.

Daniel Zook stepped back, keeping one hand on Gideon's shoulder.

His mother had both hands on his back, propelling him into the room as if she was afraid he'd turn and run out the door.

They ushered him into their narrow sitting room.

All the pretty words he'd rehearsed on the drive over had dissolved in tears. New words were crowded out by the joy filling his heart. Like the prodigal son in the Scriptures, he'd been welcomed home with love.

Mamm guided him to the couch and plopped down beside him, her hand on his arm.

Daed sat in his rocking chair. The brace on his left forearm was the only evidence he'd broken his arm.

"For twelve years we have prayed for this day." Katie Zook reached up and took off Gideon's hat. She peered at his face as if trying to memorize each line and mark age had left on him.

Gideon sat under her scrutiny, happy to have the moment to breathe and take stock himself.

Beneath her prayer Kapp, his mother's hair was the hue of old pewter. Age had dulled the green of her eyes. Her hands were softer than he remembered. Arthritis had crooked one little finger.

His father had lost most of his hair. The fringe circling his head brushed his collar in the fashion of the Amish. His thick beard hung to the middle of his chest.

Taking his mother's hand, Gideon held it tight. "I've come home to ask your forgiveness."

His mother bit her bottom lip and looked at his father. She would take her cue from him no matter what was in her heart.

Gideon looked into his father's gray eyes. Daed was a minister in the church and highly respected within the community, which made Gideon's leaving all the more hurtful.

"Can you forgive me, Daed?" The old familiar term of endearment rolled easily off his tongue. He squeezed his Mamm's hand, but continued to address his father. "I couldn't be baptized and risk *Meidung*. In truth, I knew leaving would cause a separation between us. I didn't honor you or all I was taught growing up. I am ready to make up for that now."

He waited while his father rocked in his chair, considering what Gideon had said. The seconds while he debated felt like an eternity. Then Daniel Zook leaned forward and placed his gnarled hand over his wife's and Gideon's hands. "We're glad to have you home, son."

The pressure in Gideon's chest eased. Now was the time to address the question of the money. Fear rippled anew across his sore heart. "I spoke to Abram." Gideon forced the words out. "He's angry with me."

Daniel Zook nodded. "He carries hurt too deeply."

Gideon took a shaky breath. "He thinks I stole money from you when I left."

"Nee!" His Mamm's shocked exclamation allowed a seedling of hope to take root in his heart.

His Daed frowned as the rockers on his chair creaked.

Bewildered, Gideon leaned forward in his chair. "Can you tell me why?"

"I'll tell you myself." Abram stepped into the room bringing with him the aroma of the barn.

"Abram." Mamm looked at Daed once again, waiting for him to take the lead in this conversation.

Abram didn't wait for his father to speak. He looked at Gideon, his lips in a tight line. "This is what I remember, Mamm, Daed." His hands were fisted at his sides. "After Gideon left, times were sad and hard. It shouldn't have mattered to us kids, but it did. We were children. There were no new skates under the tree. No new scooter for Joshua. We know you did your best, Mamm, knitting warm hats and mittens and scarves. But we were kids. We'd hoped for more. We'd hoped for a celebration like previous years."

Katie stared at the floor, shoulders sinking beneath the weight of Abram's words.

"Late one night after Christmas, Daed, I heard you and Mamm talking about the coming spring. You were discussing how to pay for the seed you needed to buy. I heard you say to Mamm, 'Gideon took the money.'"

The silence following Abram's words pressed in on Gideon, threatening to suffocate him. He waited for words of denial that the accusation hadn't been uttered. He couldn't look at his mother for fear her sniffling would loosen the control he had over his own heartache.

Daniel struggled up out of his chair and stood before Abram, his face gray with pain—a pain that had nothing to do with age or physical well-being. "I'm sorry you heard that, son. I'm sorry you've misunderstood all these years."

Abram remained standing, stiff and unyielding. "What misunderstanding, Daed?" The words ground out between his teeth.

Daed glanced at Gideon, an apology in his expression. "Gideon didn't physically steal money from us."

Gideon's heartache eased, but only a little.

His father appeared to look frailer than he had when Gideon first stepped through the door. "Your Mamm and I had discussed the money situation so many times I'm sure we abbreviated our words. We knew what we were saying to each other, but someone else wouldn't understand."

He turned to Gideon. "When you left, we were heartbroken. We thought we'd give you a month, maybe two, and you'd come back. You had always loved the farm and working with your hands. We couldn't imagine you'd want anything else. But when you didn't return, we hired someone to look for you. We wanted to let you know it wasn't too late—it would never be too late—to come home."

Gideon swallowed the lump in his throat. A new pain twisted beneath his ribs.

Daniel addressed Abram. "The man we hired cost a great deal of money, but if it meant finding Gideon, the expense was worth it to us. When we said, 'Gideon took the money,' what we meant was the search for Gideon took all our money. We willingly spent the money and would have spent that same money if it had been you or Joshua who had left us." Daed seemed to fold in on himself, then carefully lowered his body into the rocker.

Abram remained where he stood, staring at his father, the struggle to let go of the old pain written on his face. Finally, he looked at Gideon. "I should have asked about this matter before it became buried under years of assumptions. It just seemed like such a straightforward statement." The breath he took whistled between his teeth. His internal struggle was written in the lines on his face. "Can you forgive me, Gideon?"

Letting go of his Mamm's hand, Gideon bolted to his feet and threw his arms around his astonished brother. "We've both made mistakes that have hurt each other and the family. There is nothing left for either of us to forgive."

Abram relaxed enough to return Gideon's hug before backing away. "I'll tell Joshua the truth."

"Danke." Gideon's spirits climbed. He looked around the room at the people he loved. "I'll visit Bishop Esh again this week. I hope he doesn't make me wait too long to be baptized into the church."

The last of the ache he'd carried for so long in his heart was banished by the sparkle in his Mamm's eyes.

She rose from her chair. "I made a peach pie this morning. Would you like a slice?"

"Your peach pie is one of my favorite desserts."

She beamed and left the sitting room to go to the kitchen.

Daed continued to rock in his chair, the air of contemplation settling over him the same way it had when Gideon was a kid growing up in the household. This was the look of a minister thinking deep thoughts about the Bible and what he would preach if chosen to do so on the next church Sunday.

In the kitchen, the teakettle whistled.

Gideon helped his father out of the chair, more aware of how much he'd missed while away from his family. Thankfully, he'd returned home before either his mother or father had passed on to their heavenly reward. He still had time to reminisce about his early days growing up on the farm. And he'd been given the gift of time to make new memories to cherish in the future when his parents were no longer on this earth.

As they gathered around the kitchen table, Abram opened the conversation about the goats and Fannie.

"Have you heard from the sheriff?"

Savoring a bite of pie, Gideon shook his head. "No. Not yet. If he can't find them, it will be a devastating blow to Fannie and her aunts."

Katie stirred a splash of cream into her tea. "Why would anyone want to steal so many goats?"

"Don't know, Mamm. Maybe if we could figure that out, we'd find them before they are lost forever." Gideon cut into his pie with the edge of his fork. Bits of golden-brown crust flaked and dropped onto the plate.

Abram glanced sidelong at Gideon. "Fannie Lapp works hard caring for her aunts and their goats."

"That Lucy. She never married," Katie added.

Abram grinned, mischief dancing in his eyes. "Though there are folks who have thought it inevitable, I doubt her niece will fall to the same fate." He wiggled his eyebrows at his brother.

Gideon almost choked on the pie he was chewing. Was his attraction to Fannie that obvious? Did it really matter? He thought the world of her. He looked up to find all eyes trained on him. He cleared his throat.

"I'm not exactly what she was hoping for in a husband." He poked a peach, and it squirted juice on his plate. This sort of thing was never talked about until after the marriage was announced in the church. But he'd already proven he didn't always follow tradition, and these people were family. "I hope she'll have me anyway."

His parents looked at each other.

Daed set down his fork. "I'll speak to Bishop Esh about your next visit." His voice trembled. "I look forward to the day of your baptism. To finally have all my children welcomed into the church." He shook his head and blinked hard, not allowing the tears to fall.

Mamm's soft cheeks crinkled when she smiled. Though she looked at Gideon, she spoke to her husband. "Daniel, we'll have to take a trip to town. I need black fabric to make Gideon's wedding suit."

16

Fannie ran her hand over the clothing and towels hanging on the clothesline. The pure afternoon sunshine had dried them and they were ready to be taken indoors. Hanging the fabric bag full of clothespins close by, she removed and folded Gideon's trousers.

She wondered how his visit with his parents was going. This morning he'd struggled between leaving to visit them or staying to wait for word from the sheriff. That he wanted to be here for her lit a warm flame inside her. Knowing he cared was enough. She'd sent him on his way with her blessing.

She was glad she did. She'd jumped at every little noise hoping for news from the sheriff. First little Micah appeared at the door delivering eggs. Leland was next, coming by to check on her and leave a bucket of blueberries from his bushes. He felt terrible that the goats had disappeared on his watch and had called the sheriff to report what time he'd checked on them and found them still in the pasture.

Fannie carried the full laundry basket into the house. Gideon could take his clean trousers with him to his attic bedroom after supper tonight.

In the kitchen, her aunts were making bread. Aunt Susie was measuring cups of flour and water while Aunt Lucy kneaded another loaf.

Fannie folded dish towels at the kitchen table, engrossed in her own thoughts, only half listening to her aunts chattering back and forth in Pennsylvania Dutch. Her ears perked up when she heard Gideon's name mentioned in the bread-baking corner. Listening closer, Fannie blushed. She and Gideon had been the subject of discussion over tea at the flea market. A conversation with Bonnie Esh had raised all kinds of speculation.

Snapping a towel, Fannie looked over her shoulder. "I can hear every word you're saying over there, ya know."

The aunts looked at each other and giggled like two young schoolgirls.

Aunt Susie sprinkled flour on the counter to begin kneading her own loaf. "We're happy, 'tis all. Let us old ladies have our joy."

Fannie turned back to folding dish towels. Bonnie Esh and her aunts had grown up together. They were harmless, but she didn't like it that Gideon's decision to join the church was part of their discussion. "Visits to the bishop are no one else's concern," she scolded.

Aunt Susie bustled across the kitchen and spun Fannie around to face her.

A fine dusting of flour powdered Aunt Susie's face. The wide center part in her gray hair peeked from beneath her Kapp. Her eyes, framed by laugh lines, were a bright silver. She shook Fannie by the shoulders. "You listen to me, Fannie Lapp. If we want to dote on that boy, it is our right to do so. We're loving him back into the fold where he belongs." Susie looked at Lucy for backup. "Isn't that what Scripture says we're supposed to do, sister?"

"Jah." Her strong hands never faltered as she pounded the dough into submission. "Love never fails."

Fannie shooed her aunt away. The two of them thought they were doing God's work making a match for her. Fortunately for Fannie, the man they had chosen for her was the same man she loved.

She froze in shock, a towel hanging in the air before her.

She loved Gideon.

As if in a trance she lowered her arms and ran the thought through her mind many times, testing it for truth. She wanted to shout and laugh, but also keep the revelation hidden in her heart.

Happiness bubbled up inside her. She hadn't dared read too much into what he'd said at the barn raising. But what if he truly meant what he'd said? If he did, she should be thankful her aunts were "loving him into the fold."

A tiny sting of guilt accompanied her joy. Feeling this happy seemed wrong while struggling with the loss of her goats and Titus's poisoning.

She would accept this as a sign. Today was the beginning of good things happening to her and everyone she loved. She would rest in that and hold the joy close. She loved Gideon.

In her favorite chair in the sitting room, Fannie took out her crochet hook and yarn, and started a foundation chain. She needed to make more washcloths to wrap the next batch of soap.

Someone knocked at the kitchen door.

Setting aside her crocheting, she jumped out of her chair, hoping the sheriff had come with news.

Her cousin entered the living room.

"Good morning, Sarah." Fannie settled back with her hook and yarn.

Sarah sank into the overstuffed chair Aunt Lucy favored. "Where's Gideon?" She knotted her hands in her lap.

Praying for patience, Fannie continued to work on the washcloth. "He's visiting his parents."

"Oh." Sarah huffed. "Well. I *hope* that's where he is."

Fannie dropped her hands to her lap, her work forgotten. "What do you mean by that?" She tried to tamp down the spark of anger before it blazed hot.

Sarah smoothed her hand over her baby belly and shrugged. "He's not on good terms with his family. How can you be sure that's where he is?"

"Where else would he be?" Not recognizing her own voice, Fannie set aside her crocheting and stood up. "Come with me." Not wanting Aunt Susie and Aunt Lucy to hear what was about to transpire, she led Sarah through the kitchen.

Her aunts looked up from their bread baking and watched her stomp out the door with Sarah in tow.

Fannie didn't stop until they were in the barn.

Sarah huffed in her wake, gingerly taking a seat on the bale of hay Fannie pointed to.

Her ire close to unmanageable, Fannie stood in front of Sarah. "Tell me what you meant by that remark."

"You don't know that man like I do. He's irresponsible and unreliable. All I'm saying is how can you be so certain he's where he says he is?"

Fannie took a deep breath. "You're remembering the young man you knew twelve years ago. What kid isn't irresponsible and unreliable sometimes, especially during the running-around years?"

"Why are you defending him?" Sarah shook her finger at Fannie. "I warned you about him. He hoodwinked Mamm into hiring him."

Ignoring Sarah's pointed finger, Fannie continued. "He has worked hard around here. Have you asked Samuel about all he's done to help him?"

Sarah fiddled with her apron. "I haven't." The mutinous set of her jaw was evidence she wasn't ready to give up the fight.

Fannie pressed on. "From all I've seen and heard, they work well together. Samuel wouldn't put up with a slacker. You ought to know that better than I. He'd be the first to come and tell Aunt Susie she'd made a mistake." Out of breath and shocked she'd had the courage to speak her mind, Fannie paused.

Sarah took the opportunity to jump in. "You've fallen in love, Fannie." She made it sound like a death sentence.

The heat of a blush raced across Fannie's cheeks remembering what she'd only admitted to herself earlier in the kitchen.

Detecting weakness, Sarah inflicted the crushing blow. "He's got you thinking about forever with him. He's more English than Amish now. He'll get bored with you and leave."

Fear knotted hard in Fannie's stomach, but she refused to give into it. "You're wrong." Her fingers rested on her scar. Hadn't he seen the bishop and bought a horse and buggy? He was visiting his family to make amends.

"Have it your way. I've warned you." Standing, Sarah brushed pieces of hay from her skirt and stalked toward the open barn door, a dark silhouette against the afternoon sunshine.

With sharp clarity, an image of Sarah and a boy flashed through Fannie's mind. A memory—there one moment and gone the next.

"Sarah." Fannie's voice sounded strained.

Sarah turned, curiosity flashing in her eyes.

"This isn't about Gideon." Fannie let her hand fall away from her cheek. She advanced on her cousin. "All your accusations, all your distrust." With each word, Fannie's voice got stronger. "This has *never* been about Gideon."

"I don't know what you're talking about." Sarah edged toward the barn door.

"What you're accusing Gideon of, what you fear he will do to me was done to you." Fannie paused, trying to recall the memory that had flashed so briefly, like light in the darkness. "Not Samuel, but someone else."

Sarah recoiled and blinked hard.

Fannie concentrated on the hazy, half-formed image in her mind. "We lived in the main house. You were eighteen. I was upstairs getting ready for bed and looked out the window. It was nighttime, but there was a light in the barn. You were standing in the barn door, like you are right now. A silhouette. There was a boy with you."

Sarah's shoulders shook with the effort to hold back tears.

Another memory clicked into place. "The next day Aunt Susie and Uncle Will were ecstatic. You had decided to be baptized." Fannie walked toward her cousin. "Who was he, Sarah?"

Shaking her head, Sarah refused to look at Fannie. "It's not important. He's not here anymore."

"It's important to you." In Fannie's mind the final piece clicked into place. *He's not here.* "Was he an Englischer? One of the local boys you met during your Rumspringa?"

Sarah paled, but stood her ground.

Confidence like she'd never felt before flowed through Fannie. "Did you love him? Did he decide an Amish girl wasn't exciting enough for him?"

Sarah's composure cracked. One tear ran down her face.

"Look at you, Sarah. You have everything, *everything* I want. A home of your own. A husband who is completely in love with you. Three precious children and another on the way. Let go of this old hurt. Live the wonderful life you have."

Sarah covered her face with both hands and sobbed.

Shocked by the depth of pain her cousin had kept hidden for so many years, Fannie wrapped Sarah in her arms and held on. "It's okay to cry."

Sarah leaned against Fannie and gave in to the anguish.

Sharing her cousin's heartache, Fannie cried with her until they were both out of tears.

Sarah sniffed and pulled back. "I d-don't want you to experience w-what I did." She scrubbed at her face. "Does that make me terrible?"

Fannie wiped her eyes on her sleeve. "No. Wanting the best for someone is never terrible."

Sarah backed away. Breathless, she tried to laugh and failed miserably. "Look at me. I'm a mess. This time you're the strong one." She lifted her apron and dabbed at her eyes. "You've changed, Fannie. Ever since Gideon came to work for Mamm."

"Maybe," she hedged, but she knew it was true. She needed time to consider what had changed. Smiling at her cousin, Fannie straightened Sarah's Kapp. "Love is a choice, Sarah. Choose love with Samuel and your babies, and with all of us who are here and love you right back."

The rumble of a large truck pulling off the road and into the farm's lane broke the afternoon quiet. Fannie looked past the Grossdawdi Haus toward Sarah's home and the big barn. "Is Samuel expecting a delivery?"

"No."

Fannie limped out of the barn. Sarah followed close on her heels.

Over the top of the emerald sea of corn, the red cab of a truck moved slowly along the lane. It pulled an aluminum box trailer. The truck drove past the big dairy barn and continued on the lane, passing Sarah's big house.

Hope filled Fannie's heart as she hurried for the gate.

After indulging in two pieces of his Mamm's pie, Gideon followed Abram into the barn. Standing in the familiar surroundings, a wave of memories crashed over him. Here on his father's farm he'd lived close to the soil. He'd learned animal husbandry, raising crops, carpentry, and a host of other skills.

Abram took him into the updated milking parlor, so different from Fannie's small goat operation. "We've increased the size of the dairy herd to sixty. We have a diesel generator to power the milking machines." He looked sidelong at Gideon. "Change comes when needed."

Gideon would need a wagonload of patience in the coming years. "Thanks for the reminder." He'd have to trust that the bishop and men like his father would make the right decisions for the good of all the people.

Leaving the barn, they walked to the carpentry shop, where compressed air was used to run the machines needed to make the gazebos and garden furniture.

"We sell locally. I want to build up inventory and have a booth at the flea market."

Gideon ran his hand over the smooth arm of a chair. "You made this?"

"Jah."

"Excellent work, Abram."

Ever the humble Amish man, his brother looked away. "I enjoy working with wood."

Leaving the woodshop, they walked down the hill to the old apple orchard. The trees were healthy, the grass beneath short and clean of any drops.

"This fall we'll sell the apples at the farm stand. I'm also considering a pick-your-own operation for all of our fruits." Abram pointed to a spot beyond the orchard to rows of bushes covered in white netting. "Those are blueberries."

He turned and pointed to the south. "I planted red raspberry canes this spring. We should have a small crop next year. Mamm keeps talking about the jam she's going to make. I hope she's able to do that."

Abram's words twanged across Gideon's heartstrings. "I was

shocked to see them so frail."

With his hands on his hips, Abram continued to stare into the distance.

"What aren't you telling me?" Gideon prodded.

"They both have health problems." Abram crossed his arms. "They started to go downhill after you left."

Gideon didn't flinch, though his brother's words felt like a spear to his heart. Had he stayed as an eighteen-year-old, he'd have been miserable, wondering what he was missing by blindly following in his father and his grandfather's footsteps. There had been no easy answers for him back then.

Gideon didn't give voice to his thoughts. He cleared the lump in his throat. "I have a lot of catching up to do."

Abram nodded and started walking again. "Diversity is key. The days when we could do only the dairying to make ends meet are gone. And Daed isn't able to help much."

The gravel wagon path leading out of the orchard crunched beneath the soles of their shoes. Gideon walked at Abram's side. His brother had given him the fifty-dollar tour. Whatever point he was trying to make, he was coming at it sideways.

Abram stopped and looked out across the field. "I want to hire someone. We don't use the cabin down on the pond anymore, so that could be housing. It'll need a lot of work first though." He faced Gideon. "What do you think of that idea?"

Gideon's thoughts raced to the future and back in the space of a second. He'd always loved the secluded cabin that had been the original homestead. "It's a *gut* idea."

"There's room for a married couple. Eventually, we could add onto that little house." Abram's eyes burned into Gideon. "Of course, I'd prefer to have family living here on the farm with us, especially in the ancestral home."

Gideon dared to crack a smile. "I think that makes the idea sound much better."

Abram nodded his head once. "*Gut*. Will we be celebrating your baptism into the church, then?"

"Jah." The life Gideon wanted began with the church. After that, a place at his Mamm's table, a place on the family farm, and a woman who held his heart in her capable hands would follow.

"Wilkum home, Bruder." Abram slung his arm around Gideon's shoulders.

On the walk back to the house, Gideon mentally ticked off what needed to be done to the old cabin while his brother rambled on about hybrid tomatoes, his oldest daughter, an upcoming auction, and half a dozen other things.

Gideon gave his brother a hug. "Don't give away that job yet."

A smile lit up Abram's previously dour face. "For you, I'll hold it."

At the Grossdawdi Haus, Gideon went in to say goodbye.

Mamm enveloped him in a hug. "You'll come back soon, jah?"

"Jah." When she let him go, he turned to his father. "Daed, I'll be speaking with Bishop Esh."

Daniel gripped Gideon's arm. "I never stopped praying you would come back. Today my prayers were answered."

"Danke for not giving up on me." With a spring in his step, Gideon left the Haus. Driving out of the yard, he glanced back.

His parents stood side by side in the doorway, waving goodbye.

A half hour later, Fiona's coat gleamed beneath the afternoon sun as she trotted down the main street of Winsome. Reining her in at Willard's Hardware store, he prayed Fannie had heard from the sheriff and the goats were on their way home. Even if the happy ending he wished for with Fannie didn't come true, the fence would still have to be fixed. He hadn't thought to ask Abram if he could bring a few goats with him to the home place.

Gideon secured Fiona to the rail. He was getting way ahead of himself. Here he was dreaming of Fannie in the cabin on the pond, and she had no clue how he felt. Well, maybe a small clue. But she certainly didn't know he was seriously thinking about marriage.

Hurrying through the store, he purchased the fencing he needed and tossed it behind the buggy seat. While he was in town, he'd check on Titus. He hoped he'd have more good news to share with Fannie.

17

Fannie fumbled the tricky latch on the gate. Intended to be goat-proof, at this moment the latch was also Fannie-proof.

Sarah swatted her aside. "Let me do that."

Aunt Susie and Aunt Lucy appeared on the porch, drawn outdoors by the growl of the truck's engine. A vehicle this large never came this far up the lane.

"Do you think he's lost?" Fannie stood on the grassy edge of the gravel drive afraid to hope this truck might be the answer to her prayers.

"He would have stopped at the house or barn if he was lost." Sarah clutched Fannie's arm. "Stay back until he stops that thing."

Barely able to breathe, Fannie watched the truck roll to a stop. Air swooshed from the brakes, and the engine died.

A silence, heavy with anticipation, hung over the yard.

And then, she heard the sound she had longed to hear.

The soft clang of a bell, followed by the bleating of a goat.

Feet rooted to the ground, Fannie stared at Sarah, afraid to believe her ears. She'd prayed so hard for the goats to come home that she could barely believe the prayer had been answered. Her breath seized in her chest. They were *home*.

Sarah giggled and squeezed Fannie's arm before pushing her toward the truck. "Go! Go see!"

With a shriek of joy, Fannie hurried as fast as her aching leg would carry her.

The driver's door squealed on its hinges, and a large man wearing a green cap climbed out. "This the Lapp farm?"

"Yes." Hands clutched together, Fannie looked at the aluminum trailer. "You have my goats!" She could hear their distinctive bleats. Tulip's high-pitched single note. Candytuft's rolling trill. Bluebell's low bass that sounded more like a belch.

"If you're Fannie Lapp, I have goats for you."

"All of them?" She peeked in the narrow air spaces, but tears blurred her vision and she was unable to see into the dim interior.

"Well, now. I don't know how many 'all of them' would be, but I have quite a few nannies and kids."

Wiping away tears, she listened, recognizing Daffodil's distinct screaming bleat.

The crunch of tires over gravel heralded the arrival of the sheriff. The burly man stepped from his car and ambled over.

"You are a lucky lady, Miss Lapp."

Fannie met his big grin with a smile of her own. "Jah. Thanks to you." She thought she would float away with happiness.

"Actually, it's thanks to a gentleman who heard the news of the theft and called us from a livestock auction. Your goats were ready to go up for sale."

Fannie shivered and inhaled a shaky breath looking with longing at the trailer. The bleating within grew louder.

The truck driver pulled on a pair of gloves and opened the gate into the barn with a smile. "Sounds like they're as eager to see you as you are to see them. I'll back my truck around and get them unloaded."

"Let's move out of the way." The sheriff stepped to one side.

Fannie had a different idea and darted into the barn. Her skin felt prickly with pins and needles. At last, her nannies and kids were home.

Lining up the rear of the trailer with the open gate, the driver came back around and lowered the ramp. Inside the trailer, the goats were confined in small pens to keep them from being injured on the ride.

Aunt Susie and Aunt Lucy had ventured off the porch and stood with Sarah. Aunt Susie held a small plastic bowl filled with broken pieces of oatmeal cookies.

Daffodil stuck her nose out between the bars, carrying on as if she would die if she weren't released immediately.

The driver slid two pieces of iron fence down either side of the ramp, forming a chute to guide the goats into the barn. First out was Daffodil. The doe ran straight to Fannie.

Laughing and squealing, Fannie hugged the herd queen, murmuring foolishness the entire time. Soon she stood in the center of the milling herd, being bumped on all sides and nearly deaf with the clanging of the bells and excited bleating.

Heart near to bursting, she stroked them and counted noses. One kid was missing. Someplace along the way Candytuft had lost one of her twins. Sadness filtered through Fannie's joy, tempering the air of celebration.

Aunt Susie and Aunt Lucy handed out the treats. The goats climbed over each other eager to get a bite.

"Thank you." Fannie stepped through the herd to the gate where the sheriff and truck driver stood smiling at the antics of the gamboling kids. "Thank you, both of you, so much."

"Glad to be of help." Waving goodbye, the driver got into his truck and drove away down the lane.

The sheriff watched him go before turning back to Fannie. "Thank you for calling us. I know it's not what you folks normally like to do."

Fannie looked down, unsure how to respond.

"We apprehended the thieves. Your goats weren't the only ones to disappear. There were other stolen goats there too."

Startled by that news, Fannie looked at him. "Others?"

"Yes. And because you had the courage to ask for help, no more will go missing." He held out his hand. "I'm glad you called."

She shook his hand, amazed by what her single call had accomplished. "Danke—for everything." She watched him drive away before returning to the herd.

Each goat needed a full inspection. Bluebell had a laceration on her hip. Everyone needed a good brushing, and a couple of them would have to suffer through having their legs washed. No telling what else Fannie would find after looking them over. She wished the nannies could talk and tell her where they'd been.

She led Daffodil to the grooming stand. After giving the queen a ration of grain, she set to work brushing her.

Her aunts and Sarah came into the barn and made themselves comfortable on bales of hay. They had come to watch Fannie work, but the nannies had other ideas. Happy to be home, they stuck like burrs to their people, nudging and bumping and begging for attention.

Fannie collected extra brushes and gave one to each of the aunts. "Sit right there on the bale of hay and brush whoever or whatever you can reach."

"What about me?" Sarah held out her hand.

Fannie stood with her mouth agape. Sarah? Brush a goat? "Are you sure?"

Her cousin looked nervously at the animals all around her. "They won't bite, will they?"

"They might try and taste your sleeve, but they won't bite." Fannie couldn't fully comprehend having this conversation. With *Sarah*. Unbelievable.

"Then let me have the brush you're holding." Sarah took it and gingerly ran it across Tulip's back.

"Stay seated." Of all times for Sarah to decide she wanted to do barn chores. She was about to have a baby for goodness' sake. *Mercy!*

"I will. Go do what you have to do." Sarah turned her full attention to wielding the brush.

Baffled by this new Sarah, Fannie took Daffodil into the milking parlor, where she could feed the doe a ration of grain while examining her from nose to tail.

Pleased with the overall condition of her goats, Fannie was sitting on a small stool, finishing her inspection of Tulip when something cold touched the back of her neck. She whirled about and came face to nose with—*Titus!*

Squealing with happiness, Fannie threw her arms around his neck and hung on.

The big dog wore a silly grin. His tail waved high over his back, a plume of happiness.

"Oh, Titus." She buried her nose in his ruff and let her tears flow into his fur. She'd been so afraid he would die. "How'd you get here?"

He gave a deep *woof* and licked her ear.

"I brought him home."

Fannie's heart bounced at the sound of Gideon's voice.

Gideon stood in the milking parlor doorway, his throat aching around the baseball size lump stuck there. As if the time with his family hadn't taxed his emotions enough for one day, witnessing Fannie and her herd guardian's happy reunion tested them some more. He rubbed the back of his neck and willed away the moisture in his eyes.

Titus wagged his tail as Fannie fawned over him.

And, no, that wasn't a stab of jealousy in his gut. *Get a grip, Zook.*

"He's fully recovered?" Fannie had lifted her head out of the dog's thick ruff.

Gideon rubbed his hand across his eyes and took a deep breath. "Doc Silva didn't detect any organ failure, but he wants us to keep a close watch on him the next few days."

"That's *gut.*" She hugged Titus, rubbed his chest, and scratched his rump. All of which put the big dog into a state of drooling bliss. "I won't let him out of my sight!"

"I see the goats came home." He hid his surprise at seeing the aunts and Sarah brushing goats. "It looks like a beauty parlor out there."

"They were dirty. Someone called the sheriff from the livestock auction."

Even though the goats were safely home and in her care, Gideon detected a lingering note of shock in her voice. "A good Samaritan to the rescue. Everybody okay?"

"A few cuts and scrapes." Fannie unhooked Tulip from the milk stand.

Eager to rejoin the herd, the goat dashed past Gideon and into the barn's loafing area.

Titus followed the doe out of the parlor, already back on duty.

"We lost one kid." Fannie set aside a tube of ointment.

Gideon pulled her up into his arms and held her tightly. "I'm sorry to hear that, Fannie."

She rested her cheek against his chest and slid her arms around him. "It's hard losing one, but I have so much to be thankful for."

He strained to hear her whispered agreement, marveling again at how right she felt in his arms.

"The sheriff thanked me for calling." She looked up at him, wonder in her voice. "They were able to rescue other goats too, not just mine."

"Oh. I'm sorry." They jumped apart as Sarah, in the doorway between milk room and parlor, turned away and went back towards the barn.

Fannie's eyes were huge in her pale face.

Fearing she would run away, Gideon rested his hands on her shoulders and said, "Breathe."

She looked at the empty doorway and back at him. "I-I . . . Oh, Gideon." The heat of embarrassment flamed across her cheeks. Her hand at her cheek, she refused to meet his gaze.

"Look at me, Fannie."

She glanced at him and away.

He refused to let go of her until her gaze returned to his. "We are not in a public place, and what Sarah saw doesn't require public confession by any stretch of *your* imagination." He waggled his eyebrows at her.

Laughter sputtered from Fannie's lips. "Public confession?"

"Well, the way you act, a person would think that." He wanted to point out he hadn't gotten to the good part—a kiss. But he decided not to press his luck. That would surely send her racing for the house. "C'mon. Let's go find Sarah." He took her hand, ignoring the horror on her face. "Let's see what she wanted."

With her hand on her cheek and dragging her feet, Fannie followed. "I can't face her."

"Yes, you can." He almost reminded her Sarah was a married woman, but decided that might hurt his cause. Stepping into the barn, he stopped abruptly.

Sarah sat on a bale of hay between her mother and Lucy, her hand covering her face. What he could see of her face was bright red.

Smiles big as all of Pennsylvania, Susie and Lucy looked up at him.

Great. An audience. He didn't care, but Fannie . . . He looked down at her snug against his side. His view consisted of the top of her head covered by her Kapp. He'd concentrate on one person at a time. "Sarah."

She peeked at him over her splayed fingers. "I'm sorry." Her eyes turned toward Fannie. "Don't look so terrified, Fannie." Taking a shaky breath, she dropped her hand. "I'm getting ready to go home and wanted to say goodbye."

Fannie stood frozen in place.

Gideon leaned down and prompted her with a whisper. "Say goodbye."

Taking a deep breath, Fannie finally looked at Sarah. "Danke for helping with the goats." Clinging to Gideon, she whispered to him, "You have no idea how amazed I am to be saying that."

"What?" he whispered back.

"Sarah and goats in the same breath." She couldn't believe it.

"Oh."

"Hey." Sarah crossed her arms. "I can brush a goat as well as Mamm or Aunt Lucy."

Her mother and aunt giggled.

Fannie grinned. "Danke, Sarah." She paused, and then said, "Goodbye."

Sarah stood up. "Be happy, Fannie." She started to walk away, then turned back. "Mamm? Aunt Lucy? Time to go in now."

"I'm fine right here." Lucy beamed up at Gideon and Fannie.

Beside her, Susie settled more comfortably on the bale of hay.

Being stonewalled by two elderly Amish women wasn't something Gideon knew how to handle. While trying to decide what to say to move them along, Fannie spoke up.

"Your bread dough will be climbing out of the bowl."

"Oh!" Lucy sprang up so fast she startled Candytuft into making a giant leap across the backs of the other goats. "My bread!" She rushed out of the barn, followed by Susie.

Sarah smiled and followed them out. With a quick wave and a wink, she closed the barn door behind her.

Holding Fannie close, Gideon said, "What just happened?"

Fannie stared at the closed barn door, the beginnings of a smile curving her lips. "Sarah and I talked."

"*Gut*. That must have been some talk." Maybe one day she'd share what they talked about. He squeezed her hand. "Seems to be a day for talking."

She faced him with a bright smile. "I think it's the perfect day for talking."

18

Gideon rolled up the hose and put away the mop. The afternoon sun slanted through the window, shining a spotlight on Fannie as she wiped down the sink in the milking parlor. The light captured glints of red and gold in the tiny curl that had escaped her Kapp and lay against her nape.

She glanced up at him. "How was your visit with your parents?"

Gideon set aside the bucket. His heart was full to overflowing with all that had happened today. "I had an amazing day, Fannie. They welcomed me home with open arms, like the prodigal son in the Bible." Gideon wiped his eyes on his sleeve. "My eyes have been real watery today." He looked at Fannie. The soft understanding in her brown eyes warmed his heart.

She smiled shyly. "It must be the season. My eyes have done their fair share of watering too."

They both laughed.

He was unable to stop smiling. To share the rest of his life with someone who made him laugh would make the journey so much better.

Gideon took a deep breath. "When I first left home twelve years ago, my Mamm and Daed were looking for me." The wonder of that continued to strike a chord of relief in him. They had never once given up on him. "The man they hired to find me was expensive, which accounted for the lean years. Abram misunderstood something he overheard them say. That's why he thought I stole their money."

"Does Abram know he misunderstood?"

She wasn't going to let it go. Her dear heart wanted everyone to have a happy ending, and Gideon wanted to give it to her.

"He does. Mamm and Daed explained everything to him."

Talking to Fannie made the reality of what had transpired finally hit home. It dug deep into his heart and left him feeling so relieved his knees were weak. He leaned against the counter and took a deep breath. "Abram said he would tell Joshua."

Her shoulders relaxed, and she heaved a great sigh. "That is wonderful news, Gideon."

"Now that I've mended my relationship with my family, I'll visit Bishop Esh. It's time I took the necessary steps to be baptized into the church."

Her eyes shone with a happy light like he'd never seen. "That is *gut*, Gideon."

When he'd arrived at this little goat farm, he'd been hoping to rebuild his life with his family and the church. He hadn't expected to find love too. "I have to fix the fence, but first, come walk with me?" He held out his hand.

Her smile warmed his heart as she took his hand. Happiness radiated from her.

Today God's goodness and mercy had poured an abundance of love into his life.

Fannie's heart thundered loud in her ears as Gideon wrapped her hand in his. She followed him out of the barn, breathless with anticipation. Beneath the brim of his hat, a light shone in his eyes the likes of which she'd never before seen.

"Fannie, are you still uncertain I'm making the right choice returning to Winsome?"

She bit her bottom lip in an effort to stop it from trembling, but it was no use. She couldn't bite her lip and talk at the same time. "I think you will do what you put your mind to."

He nodded as though satisfied with her answer. "*Gut.*" He hesitated, then asked, "You love your aunts a great deal. Have you ever thought of leaving them for a home of your own?"

Fannie lifted her hand to her mouth in shock. Did he think she'd never thought of such a thing? Having her own home and family was her most precious dream!

His eyes lit with determination, he kept going. "You see, when I spoke with Abram today, I found out all the things he's been doing on my Daed's farm."

He led her past Aunt Lucy's herb garden and between Aunt Susie's flower beds toward the porch. The smell of baking bread wafted through the open window.

"The work on the farm is more than he can handle. There's a small cabin on the pond, and he offered it to me if I want to fix it up."

At the unexpected turn in the conversation, Fannie's heart fell and landed painfully on her toes. "You're leaving us to go work for him?" She couldn't stop the tears from forming in her eyes.

"No. I mean, yes. I mean, you'd come with me. If you wanted to." He dragged in a deep breath. "I'm making a mess of this. Let me start again." He cleared his throat and looked at her. "I'm sorry. I'm not your traditional Amish man."

Fannie blinked back the tears and tried to listen with her heart. Tightening her grip on his hand, she pulled him to a stop. "Maybe that's a *gut* thing. Aunt Susie says I need to stretch my views."

His mouth hung open for a moment before he clapped it closed.

She jumped back when he fell to one knee.

He took off his hat and set it on the porch step. "I love you, Fannie. Will you marry me?"

His words came out in such a rush, her comprehension lagged by a few seconds. Tears welled with the realization of what he'd asked her. Her heart near bursting, Fannie swayed. He helped her sit on the step.

She stared up at him, speechless. For so long she'd dreamed of this moment. She finally understood what Aunt Susie and Prudy had been trying to tell her about love. It didn't matter how she thought it should come to her, or what she thought it would look like. Love would always surprise.

A worried frown on his face, Gideon sat on the step beside her. "Your aunts hoped the accident at the barn raising would bring us together. In truth, it was your fall the first day I came to work here. Do you remember? The goats were getting the better of you."

Fannie nodded, wanting to tell him she loved him too. But he kept talking, and she didn't have the ability to speak quite yet.

"I lifted you up, and I fell—head over heels in love with you." He grinned sheepishly. "Of course, it took some time for me to realize what had happened. Partially because there was a stubborn Amish girl raising questions and making me think more carefully about my decision to return."

Fannie felt the warmth of a blush on her cheeks. Finally, she said quietly, "You are the perfect Amish man for me, Gideon Zook." She coasted her fingers across the scar on her cheek. He was no longer the youth of her girlish fantasies. Gideon was an interesting and complex man. Marriage to him would be the adventure of a lifetime. She peeked at him from beneath her lashes and lowered her hand away from her scar. "I love you too. I'd be honored to be your wife."

Something warm and soft unfurled in Fannie's chest. Love had given her the wings she'd always wanted. Not for her feet, but for her heart.

He leaned toward her and kissed her lips. Then he sprinkled kisses across the scar on her cheek.

From the open sitting room window came the sound of giggling and clapping hands.

"This calls for an extra-special Tay with rose petals, I think, sister," she heard Aunt Lucy say.

Gideon looked at Fannie and grimaced, then burst into laughter and hugged her close.

Nestled in the warmth of his arms, Fannie saw her future shining in the light of his eyes.

Gideon lowered his lips to hers.

Fannie closed her eyes and let her heart soar.

Up to this point, we've been doing all the writing. Now it's *your* turn!

Tell us what you think about this book, the characters, the plot, or anything else you'd like to share with us about this series. We can't wait to hear from *you*!

Log on to give us your feedback at:
https://www.surveymonkey.com/r/HeartsOfAmish

Annie's® FICTION